Praise for

A Day with a Perfect Stranger

"Brilliant. Masterful. Filled with liberating truth."

—STEPHEN ARTERBURN, best-selling author of *Every Man's Battle,* founder and chairman of New Life Ministries

"Don't let David Gregory's simple writing style fool you: the message shared throughout *A Day with a Perfect Stranger* is profound, and the questions he raises are life changing."

—LIZ CURTIS HIGGS, best-selling author of *Bad Girls of the Bible*

"Fasten your seat belt for another marvelously divine encounter with the *Perfect Stranger*! Once again, Gregory masterfully demonstrates just how passionately and intimately our God loves each one of us. If you are looking for an encouraging faith encounter, the *Perfect Stranger* books are the most palatable and powerful tools of our day."

—SHANNON ETHRIDGE, best-selling author of *Every Woman's Battle* and *Every Woman's Marriage*

"While I liked *Dinner with a Perfect Stranger* very much, I *loved A Day with a Perfect Stranger.* This book has the potential to make people think about what drives them, what keeps them from God, and what will ultimately fulfill them. In a feelings-based and satisfaction-driven society, this is an invaluable tool. People are hungering for the answers to questions Mattie gets to ask. I can't wait to hand it out to friends who do not yet know the Stranger in their midst."

—LISA TAWN BERGREN, best-selling author of *The Begotten*

"Sometimes the simplest books can have the most profound influence, and David Gregory has done such a wonderful job capturing my imagination. Over and over as I read *A Day with a Perfect Stranger,* I kept asking myself, what would I say if I ever sipped lattes with Jesus? And at the end of the book, I realized I have that opportunity every day. He's not only listening, but he's speaking too. Anyone who enjoyed *Dinner with a Perfect Stranger* will love the sequel."

—RENE GUTTERIDGE, best-selling author of *BOO* and *The Splitting Storm*

a Day with a Perfect Stranger

a Day with a Perfect Stranger

DAVID GREGORY

WATERBROOK
PRESS

A Day with a Perfect Stranger
Published by WaterBrook Press
12265 Oracle Boulevard, Suite 200
Colorado Springs, Colorado 80921
A division of Random House, Inc.

The events and characters (except for Jesus Christ) in this book are fictional, and any resemblance to actual events or persons is coincidental.

10-Digit ISBN: 1-4000-7242-5
13-Digit ISBN: 978-1-4000-7242-2

Library of Congress Cataloging-in-Publication Data
Gregory, David, 1959-
A day with a perfect stranger / David Gregory. — 1st ed.
p. cm.
ISBN 1-4000-7242-5
1. Jesus Christ—Fiction. 2. Imaginary conversations. 3. Married women—Fiction. I. Title.
PS3607.R4884D39 2006
813'.6—dc22
2006002836

Printed in the United States of America
2007

10 9 8 7 6 5 4 3 2

Special Sales
Most WaterBrook books are available in special quantity discounts when purchased in bulk by corporations, organizations and special interest groups. Custom imprinting or excerpting can also be done to fit special needs. For information, please e-mail SpecialMarkets@WaterBrookPress.com or call 1-800-603-7051.

For Barbara,
whose soul is satisfied

My thanks to Michael Svigel and Ava Smith
for their special contributions to this book.

one

I NEVER THOUGHT I'd become the kind of woman who would be glad to leave her family. Not that I wanted to abandon them, exactly. I was just glad to get away for a few days. Or longer, in the case of one of them.

Maybe I should have been celebrating instead of escaping. That's what you do with big news, isn't it? And we had had plenty.

A few weeks earlier my husband, Nick, told me that he had met Jesus. Not the usual "getting saved" kind of meeting Jesus. I mean, met Jesus. Literally. At a local Italian restaurant.

At first I thought he was joking, of course. He wasn't. Then I thought he had been hallucinating. He had, after all, been putting in seventy-hour weeks at work and getting limited sleep. But he stuck to his story, which left me with—I didn't know what.

All I knew was that my husband was convinced he had dined with Jesus, and he had turned into some kind of Jesus freak. It was bad enough that he had previously disappeared into his work. Now when we were together, God was all he wanted to talk about. That wasn't the "till death do us part" I had planned on.

Things had been strained enough between us without bringing God into the mix. It was as if someone had kidnapped the real Nick and replaced him with a religious Nick clone. There we were, plugging along in our marriage, and suddenly Nick, who wouldn't have been caught dead in a church parking lot, is best friends with deity.

It's not that I object to religion. People can believe whatever they want to. I just didn't grow up religious, hadn't become religious, and didn't marry someone religious. And I wanted it to stay that way.

So getting away from Nick for four days was a relief. What I hated was leaving Sara, my two-year-old. Granted, I looked forward to the break, as any mother would. But I had never been away from her longer than two nights, and even then I found myself missing her by the second day. And that was with my mom coming down to take care of her. At least I trusted my mom. No telling what might happen with Nick doing the childcare. Not that he was a bad dad, when he was both home and off his cell phone.

But I had to take this trip. A client had built a resort hotel near Tucson and wanted me to design new brochures for it. The manager insisted on giving me a personal tour of the place. She said I needed to experience it firsthand to fully capture its essence. And get a free massage, I hoped.

I rarely had to travel for my graphic arts work, which was fine with me. Most of the business I had developed since we'd moved to Cincinnati was local. Sometimes I went back to Chicago on a job, but I could handle most of my old accounts online. This, however, was my biggest client—had been for six years—and I couldn't exactly say no.

The trip should have been a one-day there-and-back. Two at the max. But since you can't get a nonstop from Cincinnati to Tucson, I booked my flight through Dallas, which meant I had to take two travel days.

I could hardly imagine a less appealing way to spend two days of my life. I don't much like air travel, anyway. I'd rather just throw some stuff in the car and hit the road. In a car no one has you stand in line or searches your purse or forces you to eat dry pretzels for a snack. Nor does anyone pull you aside, have you extend your arms, and run a baton all over your body. Why do I always get singled out?

Plus, I didn't feel the best this particular morning. I knew that getting on a plane without any breakfast wasn't a brilliant idea since they don't even serve those tasteless meals anymore. But I figured I could break down and buy a snack box if I had to.

Before heading out the front door, I wrote a note and left it on the kitchen counter.

Nick,
Sara's pajamas are in the top drawer, if you don't remember. You may not, since you haven't put her to bed this year. Her toothbrush is in the left drawer in her bathroom. I left plenty of juice, oatmeal, and cereal for breakfasts. Plus she likes toast and jelly. There's a macaroni casserole she likes in the fridge and some frozen veggies. After that runs out, she likes Chick-fil-A. Don't forget story time at the library tomorrow at 10:30.

You can reach me on my cell if you need me for anything about Sara. Hope you and Jesus have a great time together.
Mattie

I drove myself to the airport. Nick had volunteered to take me, but I declined. Riding by myself was preferable to Nick telling me about his latest discovery in the Bible, which he was now reading voraciously, or listening to Christian radio, a fate worse than death. I parked and walked into the terminal. The soft music and absence of Jesus talk provided a welcome relief.

Miraculously, I made it through security without any special groping and proceeded to my gate. Once there, I sat with my carry-ons and glanced at my boarding pass. *Oh, great,* I thought. *An E seat, in the middle. Why didn't I make my reservation earlier and get a better seat? Maybe I can switch to an aisle seat near the back of the plane.*

A minute later the agent at the gate picked up her microphone and announced, "Ladies and gentlemen, our flight to Dallas is full. To expedite your departure, please make sure you stow your bags and take your seat as quickly as possible."

Fabulous.

She then started hawking two two-hundred-dollar travel vouchers for anyone willing to take a flight four hours later. No one took them. When the offer went up to three hundred dollars, I stepped forward. *Maybe they'll have an aisle seat on the next flight.*

"When would that get me into Tucson?" I asked.

The agent looked up the connecting flight. "Ten twenty-two this evening."

Nearly ten thirty. Plus taking a shuttle out to the hotel. That's after eleven.

I decided to pass; I'd be too tired the next day.

As they called first-class passengers to board, I remembered something I'd forgotten to tell Nick. I pulled out my phone and dialed his office. He answered.

"Nick, I'm at the airport."

"Hey. How's it going?"

"Look, I forgot to tell you that Laura has Sara with their son Chris until about five thirty. She's taking them swimming at the Y."

"No problem. I'm going to get home a little early and fix something for Sara and me."

"What—you mean cook something?"

"Yeah. I'm picking up stuff for spaghetti and meatballs."

"Miracles never cease. Look, I need to go—my row is boarding."

"Call me tonight?"

"I'll see, Nick. I might be pretty tired."

"Well, have a great trip. I love you."

"Yeah. Bye, Nick."

I picked up my tote bag and suitcase and got to the boarding line just as my group was being called. I walked down the ramp and waited interminably while all the people already on the plane decided where to put their stuff. By the time I got to my row, there was room overhead for my suitcase but not my tote bag. I stowed my suitcase and looked at my seating arrangement on the left. The seats on both sides of mine were already occupied. Two guys. *Great. Sandwiched for the next two and a half hours between two men. Why couldn't they have put me between two size 2 women?* The man in the aisle seat stood up to let me by. I squeezed into the middle seat, resigning myself to not having an armrest available to me on either side. Guys always hog those.

I leaned down, stuffed my bag under the seat in front of me, and pulled my shoulders inward to squeeze back into my seat. *This is really going to be a fun trip.*

The temperature inside the airplane cabin didn't help. I

reached up and opened my air vent. That made things feel a little better. I leaned back and sat, staring forward.

I didn't bring anything to read. What was I thinking? I should have stopped and picked up a novel in the airport. I never do that. It would have been kind of nice just to have something to escape into for a while.

I glanced through the seat pocket in front of me. *Maybe someone left a magazine in here.* But there wasn't much to choose from: a *SkyMall* catalog selling expensive gadgets that no one needed, instructions on using my seat as a flotation device in case we landed in the Mississippi River, and the monthly airline magazine. I opened the magazine and started reading an article about living on some Spanish coast. The houses were huge, the beaches white, the water crystal clear, the cliffs spectacular. *Who are they kidding? No real people live like this.*

Just then my cell phone rang. I squeezed forward, leaned down, searched through my bag, and caught it on the fourth ring. "Hello?"

"Hey, traveler. What's up?" It was my younger sister, Julie.

"Just got on the plane. Waiting to pull away from the gate."

"Did you get Sara taken care of, or do you need my help?"

"Well, theoretically she's taken care of. How Nick actually does with her, we'll see when I get back."

"What's he going to feed her?"

"He told me he's going to do some cooking."

I heard laughter on the other end. "Nick? Cook?"

"I know."

"Has he come back to earth, or is he still in the clouds?"

"Still in the clouds. He's totally flipped out on this Jesus thing."

"What are you going to do?"

"I'm not sure." I hesitated. "I called a lawyer yesterday and set up an appointment for next week."

"Mattie! You did?"

"I don't know. Maybe it's too soon. I just don't feel like I can take this anymore. I mean, things were already bad enough before Nick got religious. There's no way we're going to make it like this."

"I thought he'd been spending more time with you and Sara lately."

"Yeah. He has. I'm just not sure I want him to anymore. It's really confusing."

"Why don't you try counseling again?" she suggested. "Maybe a different therapist."

"What's the point? I mean, it's not like the last one did

much good. Besides, this is a different issue—not like Nick's workaholism. I just don't see any middle ground on this religion stuff."

I wanted to tell Julie more, but I heard an overhead announcement.

"I've gotta run," I told her. "They're telling us to shut off cell phones and all that. Can I call you tonight? I've got something else to tell you too."

"I don't know. I might be out."

"Julie, for once, don't go clubbing. It's bad news for you."

One of the flight attendants walked by and gave me the eye.

"I'll call you tonight," I said. "Be there, okay?"

"Okay."

I clicked off the phone, put it in my bag, leaned back, and closed my eyes. *I can't believe Nick and I aren't even making it to our fourth anniversary.*

The plane taxied to the runway and took off.

two

"HAVE YOU CONSIDERED the possibility that your husband might be on the right track?"

The guy to my right, in the window seat, had folded up his *Wall Street Journal* and turned slightly to face me. He looked like the typical business traveler: thirty-five or so, wearing a blue suit, a light blue shirt, and a patterned red tie. He was average size, trim, with dark hair.

"I'm sorry?"

"I couldn't help but overhear some of your conversation. Has it occurred to you that your husband might be right?"

I looked at him incredulously. I couldn't believe this perfect stranger was butting into my personal business.

"Right about what?"

"About God. About Jesus."

"What do you mean?"

"Again, I wasn't meaning to eavesdrop, but it sounds like your husband may have found God."

You were eavesdropping, and you are starting to tick me off. "The only thing my husband has found is another excuse to go off and do his own thing. And excuse me for saying so, but this is none of your business."

I turned away from him and looked straight ahead. I could sense him doing the same. We both sat silently. *This is really uncomfortable. I've never had an incident with someone on a plane. I can't believe he had the gall to say anything at all.*

He lifted the paper out of his lap and held it toward me. "I noticed you were looking for something to read. Would you like to share my *Journal*?"

"No," I responded. "Thanks, though."

He put two of its sections back on his lap and opened the third. I flipped open my airline magazine once more. After a moment he lowered his paper. "Do you mind if I ask you another question?"

I used my finger to hold my place in my magazine while I closed it. "No, I guess not," I replied, trying to maintain a level of politeness. *I'm going to regret this, I know.*

"Have you ever thought about having a personal relationship with God?"

"No." I tried to respond without any emotion. "I'm not really into religion."

"I'm not talking about religion. I'm talking about a relationship."

"You're talking about God. That's religion."

"I'm talking about knowing God personally."

"Yeah, well." I opened the magazine again. "Whatever."

"Do you believe in God?" he asked.

"Not really." I buried my head a little deeper in the magazine. *I don't want to blow up at this guy.*

"So you don't think God exists at all?"

"Who knows? Look—"

"Let's assume that he does. Then we're talking about reality, not religion, aren't we?"

I looked up at him. "As I started to say, anything that has to do with God is religion. And I don't want anything to do with it."

He locked his fingers in front of him and stared at them for a moment before looking back at me. "Okay. Let me ask this. If you were to die tonight, do you know where you would go?"

"No!"

Two people in the row in front of me turned my way.

"No," I repeated. "I don't think I'll go anywhere. I don't know if I'll go anywhere. I'm not worried about life after death. I'm just trying to make it through this life." I held my magazine up to my face and shifted my body toward the aisle.

"I know," he persisted. "I just hate to see you throw your marriage away. I think if you—"

I slammed the magazine on my lap and turned toward him.

"Look, you don't know anything about me, my marriage, or my life. But here you are, trying to cram your beliefs down my throat. The last thing I need is more God talk. I was hoping to escape that on this trip."

"Why do you want to escape from part of your husband's life?" he asked.

"Because it's not part of who I am," I snapped back. "It's not part of who I want to be or what I want my family to be. If that's who Nick wants to be, fine, but he can do it without me."

I rose out of my seat. "Excuse me."

The man by the aisle got out of his seat and let me by.

The people behind us were staring at me. I walked to the back of the plane. Both bathrooms were occupied, and a woman appeared to be waiting for the next opening. I stood with my arms crossed, steaming.

I can't believe I was talking to that guy. I might as well have invited Nick along. I can't believe he would talk to me that way. I told him how I feel about religion. And then for him to say anything at all about my marriage!

A boy came out of one bathroom, and the woman entered.

Now what am I going to do? I can't stand back here the rest of the flight. But I certainly don't want to sit next to him again. I glanced at my watch. More than an hour and a half to Dallas.

I thought through my options. It was certainly too late to ask anyone to switch seats. I looked around for the flight attendants. Both were at the front of the plane starting to serve snacks and drinks. *I really need to get something into my stomach to settle it down.* A man came out of the other bathroom; I went in. *I guess I'll just go back and read. I can ignore him. Surely he won't say anything else.*

I returned to my seat as inconspicuously as possible. "Hey," the window-seat guy said as I sat down. "I'm sorry if I made you mad. I only—"

"Sure," I said matter-of-factly. "Let's just drop it."

"Okay. I hope the rest of your flight goes well."

"I'm sure it will."

I closed my eyes, and, mercifully, he shut up.

three

MY EYES HADN'T BEEN CLOSED two minutes when I heard a child's laughter. I opened them. A little boy, about four, kept ducking his head between the seats in the row in front of me and looking back toward the man on my left, in the aisle seat. His head would appear, and the boy would make a funny face, giggle, and hide behind his seat. The third time I glanced at the aisle-seat guy. He was making funny faces back.

The game went on for a few minutes until the boy popped his head over the back of his seat. He had a plastic fire truck in his hand. "You wanna play with my truck?" he said to the man.

"Sure. That's quite a fire truck you have there. How many fires have you put out with it?"

"I don't know. About a hundred."

The boy ran the truck over the top of his seat and down its backside as far as his arm would reach, all the while making truck noises. Suddenly he disappeared again, only to pop back up with another toy. "Do you want to play with my police car?"

"Absolutely," the man replied. The boy reached out with the car, and the man took it from him. They both ran the vehicles along the top and back of the boy's seat, emitting *vroom* sounds and pretending to almost run the car and truck into each other, then avoiding collisions at the last second.

"The doors and trunk open up," the boy stated.

"They do? Let me see." The man opened each one. "What do you put in the trunk?"

"Bad guys."

"Oh. Kind of stuffy in there, don't you think?"

"No. I let them out when we get to the police station."

They played a few more minutes until the flight attendants reached us with beverages and pretzels. *Of course, pretzels.* I requested cranapple juice. The man on my left asked for some orange juice. The window-seat guy missed his chance by dozing off, which was fine with me. The attendant put ice in a cup for me, handed me the cup, and held out the cranapple can. The aisle guy took it and handed it to me.

"Thanks," I said.

"You're welcome."

He opened his juice. I did the same with my can and poured it over the ice in my cup. I noticed that he wasn't using the armrest between us. *That's a first for a guy.* I staked claim to it by sliding my elbow over.

"Where are you heading?" he asked.

"Tucson."

"Business or pleasure?"

"Hopefully both. I'm going down to a new resort hotel to get a feel for the place...take a few pictures. I've heard they have a nice spa too."

"Are you a photographer?"

I laughed. "No, hardly. I'm a graphic artist. Well, part-time. The rest of the time I'm a mother."

"Sounds like you have a job and a half. At least."

"That's the truth."

We both sipped our drinks.

"You're pretty good with kids," I remarked.

"I love them."

"Do you have any?" The man was about my age, early thirties; maybe he had one or two small ones himself.

"No physical descendants, no."

I thought that was an odd way to describe kids.

"How many do you have?" he asked.

"Just one. A daughter. She's two."

"What a great age."

I smiled. "It is. She's already putting full sentences together. I have a feeling she's going to be a real chatterbox. Yesterday we were driving along, talking about birthdays, and she asked me, 'Mommy, could I have a dinosaur cake for my birthday?' "

He chuckled. "I love how kids are so drawn to dinosaurs. It's like they were made specifically for kids' imaginations."

"Sara's dad can't wait to take her to the natural history museum in Chicago. I figure that's more a boy thing, but it looks like Sara might enjoy it. In a few years."

I opened my pretzels and ate one. *Why do I ever eat these things?*

The aisle guy spoke again. "Sorry for your encounter with our friend next to you." He nodded toward the window seat.

"Oh, well. I'll survive. I guess I'm a little testy right now."

"I can understand why."

He sipped his juice and opened his own bag of pretzels. I assumed he was referring to my marriage. Everyone within five rows now knew I had a bad marriage.

"Have you ever been married?" I asked him.

"No, not precisely," he answered.

"Engaged?"

"I'm sort of engaged now, you might say."

"No date set?"

"Not one that we've announced."

Sort of engaged? With no date? What kind of engagement is that?

"Have you been together long?"

"It depends on your time frame, but, yes, quite a while."

I stuffed the rest of my pretzels into the seat pocket in front of me and took another drink. "You never know what'll happen in marriage, I suppose." I wasn't sure if I was talking to the man or to myself.

"How so?"

"Well, you know. People never expect to have marriage problems. I mean, everyone realizes they'll have some problems, but no one expects to..."

My voice trailed off. Here I'd been shouting at the guy on the right for getting too personal, and now I was on the verge of spilling my story to this man on my left. Granted, he seemed a lot less judgmental. Still, I didn't know if I wanted to get into the whole thing. After all, I didn't know him from...the guy by the window. But sometimes we feel more comfortable talking with strangers. That's why people pour out their hearts to bartenders, isn't it? They're safe. They'll listen to your story, avoid passing judgment, and comment if you want them to. At least, that's the theory.

I decided to continue with my train of thought. Or, rather, line of questioning. "Why do guys change after they get married?"

"What do you mean?"

"I mean...you've never been married, but you're a guy."

"You might say that."

"And you must have been in relationships before." *He's engaged and decent looking.*

"I've been in relationships forever."

Okay, not that good looking.

"So what is it with men? It's like they get you to marry them, and once they've caught the prize, their real self comes out."

"And women aren't that way?"

"Yeah, we are, but it's different. It's just...different. We don't totally change."

"Is that how it seemed with your husband?"

"Yes. Absolutely. I just wish Nick could be more like he was when I met him."

"What was he like?" Somehow he asked that as if he really cared about my answer.

"He had time for me. I mean, he was in graduate school then, so he was pretty busy, but he took lots of time out of his schedule for me. And when he was with me, he was really with me. Like, emotionally. Unlike now."

"How is he now?"

"After we got married, that all changed. We'd moved to Cincinnati, and he started working longer hours at his new job, and he didn't have time for me anymore. Or to do anything around the house, like at least pick up every once in a while or clean the bathroom every other weekend, which he used to do. I mean, we were together for three years before we got married. Lived together for two. You'd think you'd know someone by then."

I took a drink and sneaked a glance at the window guy. I was feeling a bit self-conscious. We were close enough to the engines that the people in the other rows couldn't hear me, but I certainly didn't want him eavesdropping on more of my personal life. He was still sleeping, though.

"I don't know," I continued. "I suppose marriage is a gamble that way. You can't be sure what course your partner's life will take. I guess the man you marry isn't really the man you marry. We carry a certain image of the person we choose, and we expect them to be like that after the wedding. But they aren't. At least, Nick wasn't."

"So what's brought things to a head?" he asked. "Something usually does."

I paused. This was going to sound pretty stupid. No, beyond stupid. "Well, a couple of weeks ago Nick came home late one night claiming that he'd had dinner with—I'm not kidding—Jesus Christ. Completely out of the blue. I mean, he seems to have been in his right mind one day, and then the next, he's making up bizarre stories and turning into a religious nut."

"So he's giving you the same story now..."

"Exactly the same. All he can talk about now is Jesus. He's never been religious before, not in the least. I've tried to ride this out, but it's driving me crazy."

"How have things been apart from that?"

"Actually, he's been around a little more. Spent more time with me and Sara. I think he finished a project at work. But I'd almost rather go back to the way we were. This is not the man I married. I didn't plan on religion making a sudden appearance. It's messing everything up."

"Religion always messes everything up," he replied. "I hate religion."

four

AT THIS POINT in the flight I experienced my second-worst nightmare of air travel (next to being trapped by an evangelist): the guy in front of me tilted his seat all the way back. *Jerk. Where do people get off thinking they have a right to put their seats back without asking? I'm five eleven! "Excuse me for making you miserable back there, lady, but I'm much more comfortable." Oh, no problem. Now I have the choice of either doing the same to the person in back of me or being transported to Dallas in a space half the size of my car trunk.* I resisted the urge to do what I always want to do, which is to nonchalantly dig my knees into the person's seat until they straighten back up.

I finally decided to put the issue out of my mind—my stewing wasn't affecting the guy in front of me in the least—

and get back to the man in the aisle seat. I wondered about his last comment, about religion. I had mixed feelings about delving further into it. I was already struggling enough with my feelings toward Nick's new diversion; I didn't know if I needed to egg them on. But I was curious as to his opinion.

"Why do you dislike religion?"

"Don't you?"

"Well..." Asked to provide an actual answer, I realized that wasn't so simple. I always said that people could believe whatever they wanted to and it didn't make any difference to me. Right now, though, I wanted to get as far away from religion as I could. "Maybe so. I'm not saying people don't have a right to believe what they want to. It's just not for me."

I poured the rest of my juice before resuming. "But what about you? You were the one who said you didn't like it."

"It keeps a lot of people from living life to the fullest," he answered. "It makes some people feel guilty over things they shouldn't feel guilty about and others worry about things they shouldn't worry about."

"I know! Religious people are so uptight."

He continued. "People spend their time doing things to placate some supposed deity. Unfortunately, it's wasted effort."

"You would think they would focus on feeding the poor or something."

"They often do. And that's a good thing. But so much of religion... People think that wearing special clothing or dipping themselves in a certain river or repeating specific religious phrases or abstaining from certain foods or traveling to specific sites earns them points. They do these kinds of things all over the world. American Christians have had their favorite rules: don't play cards, don't dance, don't go to movies—"

"Don't touch alcohol," I added. "We invited a few neighbors over one night for dessert, and one of the couples wouldn't touch the rum cake. Honestly, I was offended."

He laughed. "What's on the inside is what matters, not the external rituals."

"Totally," I agreed.

"Like the burka that some Muslim women are forced to wear."

"Is that the full covering that has slits for the eyes?"

"Right, the full covering. Most Muslim women want to dress modestly, and that's admirable. But many Muslim women are threatened or beaten for not having everything completely covered. That's evil. The men are afraid the women will make them lust. But you could put a woman in concrete blocks, and men would still lust."

I smiled. *I like this guy. He sees it like it is and tells it like it is too.*

"The problem," he continued, "is what's inside men's hearts, not what's on women's bodies. Controlling women is just an excuse for men to exercise their dominance."

"I despise that," I said. "And it seems like some people want to do the same things here! There's a church on our side of town that I heard doesn't even let women speak. I've felt like going there one Sunday morning and standing up in the middle of the service and giving them a piece of my mind."

He returned to the broader theme. "It angers me that religion has been used to justify such immense evil—slavery, racism, wars, oppression, discrimination. I hate that religion is the cause of so much ignorance and superstition in the world. I can't stand that religion is something people feel they have to escape from to lead normal lives."

"Yeah," I answered meekly as Nick popped back into my mind.

"Back where I grew up," he said, "religion and hypocrisy went hand in hand. I abhor people claiming to be one thing but in their hearts and actions being the exact opposite. I saw that all the time. The leaders just focused on the rules, which made them self-righteous. Then they would lay the rules on other people, who felt guilty when they couldn't keep them well enough. It was a big power play, a way for the leaders to keep themselves in positions of control."

"Where did you grow up?"

"In the East, in a small town."

"I've heard that small towns can be bad that way."

A flight attendant came by with a plastic bag for trash. I handed her my can but kept my cup, which had a little ice left. "Could I get some water?" I asked her.

"Of course," she said, her accent apparent. "I'll be right back with it."

In a moment she returned with a bottle of water and handed it to me. As she did, the aisle guy said something to her in a foreign language—maybe from Eastern Europe. Her face lit up, and she responded to him in kind. They conversed for a couple of minutes before she departed for the rear of the plane.

"You spoke that well," I commented. "What language was it?"

"Croatian."

"That's pretty obscure."

"I've spent some time there." He took the final sip of his

juice. "One of the things I dislike the most is when people who really do mean well get distorted by religion."

That was my biggest fear with Nick. Despite working too much, he really wasn't a bad guy. Until now, potentially.

"How do you mean?" I asked.

"People end up feeling they have to do certain things or be a certain way to be acceptable. So they stop being who they are, and instead they try to keep a bunch of rules that they can't keep, and all the time they feel guilty and miserable."

"It makes me miserable just thinking about it."

"Then they start distancing themselves from people they have meaningful relationships with. They're afraid that people who don't believe like they do will lead them astray. So instead of making them more loving, religion isolates them from the people they really do love."

I opened my water and took a long drink, then slowly screwed the cap back on. "I had a friend like that. My best friend in high school, Melinda. We had known each other since elementary school, but in high school we were on the volleyball team together, and we really got close. During our sophomore and junior years we did everything together. Then the summer before our senior year she became a Christian. Some church camp she went to."

"And after that?"

"After that our friendship was never the same. She started hanging around all her new Christian friends, and she did the Christian youth group thing, and she just didn't have much to do with me. I mean, we were still on the team together, and we still did some things, but it got less as the year went on. As a seventeen-year-old, I felt really left out."

"That's a shame," he said. "And it's exactly what I'm talking about."

"Yeah. I just knew we'd be friends forever. But I don't think we ever got together after graduation. I saw her at my ten-year reunion."

"What was she doing?"

"She had married some guy in college, and then they got divorced. I guess religion didn't help her much after all. No kids. She was dating some new guy at the time, and she was still doing her church stuff."

I unscrewed the cap of my water again and took another drink. He adjusted his body slightly to face me a little more.

"You're afraid your husband is going to do the same thing, aren't you? If not leave physically, at least emotionally."

I was surprised at his forwardness. "What are you, a counselor or something?"

"Actually, yes."

"Oh. I—"

"I didn't mean to be presumptuous. It just seemed like a similar situation."

"Yeah," I said, looking down toward my feet. "I got over Melinda after a while. High school friends, you never know. As for Nick..." I bit my upper lip to stop the tears that were welling up. "It's one thing to lose a girlfriend..."

I stared emptily for a moment. "First a workaholic, now a Jesus-aholic. Either way, Nick's not invested in me. What's the point of being married?"

"It doesn't sound like you really want to get a divorce."

"No." I surprised myself by how definite that sounded. "No, I don't. I want our family to stay together. But Nick is pulling it apart. Why is he doing that? Why did he try to get so close to me before we got married, but since the 'I do,' he doesn't really seem to care? I married to have a soul mate, not just to wear a ring and reheat dinners when Nick comes home late from work. Maybe most men grow distant like that."

He sighed. "A hard question. It depends on the guy. But mostly, men are afraid of being close. They weren't taught how to be close growing up. They weren't loved for who they are but instead for how they performed. They feel insecure and inadequate, and they don't want anyone to know them like they think they know themselves. They're afraid of being rejected."

"So instead they do the rejecting. Faultless logic that men have."

He shook his head slightly. "I wouldn't say they think through it on a logical basis at all. They naturally gravitate toward those things that make them feel competent and less susceptible to rejection, like work. They think these things will meet their soul's needs. They're wrong, but that's what they do."

"You're saying what they really need is intimacy, not work and sports and whatever."

"Work is important to a man. Very important. Providing for a family and feeling capable are part of who he is. But, yes, deep down, men want connection, just like women. They want to be loved for who they are, not what they produce. They want to feel accepted."

"So how does that relate to Nick's Jesus thing? I mean, this isn't the same as work is for him. He's not getting accolades for talking about Jesus."

"No, you're right," he answered. "This is completely

different. Nick's tapping into something deeper. If he listens well, he'll fulfill what his heart is really looking for."

"How is this going to give him what he's looking for?"

"That's the key question, isn't it? If you figure that out, you might save your marriage."

five

"IF YOU FIGURE that out, you might save your marriage."

The man's words kept running through my head. Maybe he was right. Maybe my reaction to Nick's stuff was so knee-jerk that I hadn't taken the time to look beneath the surface. Not that I much wanted to, especially this particular surface. Couldn't it have been something else? Anything else?

Exploring why Nick was having an affair might have been easier. But if my marriage was going down the drain, the least I could do was try to understand it. I knew that the Jesus thing might just be a phase, but there had to be something underneath that had led him to embrace this stuff.

The little boy popped his head back over the seat. He was apparently heading to some beach, given the ensuing discussion with the man about sandcastles and moats and building defenses against the waves.

I picked up my airline magazine again and leafed through it. I glanced at an article on Texas wines that didn't interest me much. A couple of pages on Hilary Swank's acting career wasn't a lot better. *Why don't they ever have interesting articles in these things?* I guessed they didn't want to risk offending any fliers and had to water down their content to a bland lowest common denominator. I made another halfhearted attempt to find a piece that would grab my attention but failed. I put the magazine back in the seat pocket.

I looked out the window to see where we were. Down below, a patchwork of crops covered mostly flat land. That meant we were...somewhere between Ohio and Texas. A lot of good that did me. I glanced at my watch. *Thirty-five more minutes.*

I closed my eyes. Even though my body felt drained, I wasn't exactly tired. I just didn't have anything else to do. The man in the window seat started snoring lightly. That wasn't going to make the time pass more quickly. In front of me, I heard the boy's father offer him a snack. *Typical father. Has no clue about circumstances offering him a parenting break. If the kid was being entertained by the guy next to me, why divert him?*

I tried to purge my mind and relax, but it wouldn't purge. *"If you figure that out, you might save your marriage."* The thought kept pressing in on me. *I can either let events take their course, or I can try to be proactive about my marriage. I can try to figure out and relate to what's going on with Nick. Okay, maybe not relate to it but at least understand what's happening with him. If I can understand it, maybe I can do something about it.*

I felt a small sense of resolve awaken within me. *Things may be hopeless, but I don't have to let my marriage go down without a fight. I owe that to myself, and I owe it to Sara.*

I couldn't bring myself to think that I owed it to Nick. Given his performance as a husband, he owed me, big time. But at the moment, that wasn't the point.

Why would Nick suddenly turn religious? Nick's a bright guy. Why would he believe that stuff? Or need it? Nick isn't looking for a crutch in life.

I thought back over our relationship. Had Nick ever showed any sign of taking this direction? He had gone to church occasionally growing up, I remembered, but that was because his mother made him. He couldn't stand it and didn't believe any of it. He may have had a basic belief in God, but it was pretty minimal, and it didn't mean much to him. A couple of times Jehovah's Witnesses had come to our house. He virtually slammed the door in their faces. He ridiculed the church down the street and their transparent attempts to subtly proselytize the neighbors. He never showed the slightest interest in the New Age stuff some friends of ours had gotten into—except as something for us to laugh about together.

Nick was about as nonreligious as they come. He worked. And worked. And worked. And when he didn't work, he played golf, watched football, and listened to sports talk on the radio. God didn't appear anywhere on his radar screen.

It was like I woke up one morning and a new man was drinking coffee at the breakfast table. Did he decide that work wasn't doing it for him anymore? Actually, he had been working somewhat less lately. But why turn into a Jesus freak? I would have expected him instead to spend more time on the golf course.

The truth was, Nick's direction the last several weeks simply baffled me. It had come out of nowhere. It just didn't make any sense to me. Until I momentarily entertained one far-fetched possibility.

Maybe something did happen to him. No...that can't possibly be true. But overnight Nick went from being completely nonreligious to being a religious nut. He wouldn't have just decided on his own to do that one day. Would he? It doesn't fit him at all.

What happened to him? Is it possible that somehow he really did encounter God, or whoever? But what would that even mean?

I heard the familiar airplane *ding* and glanced up to see the seat-belt sign had come on. The flight attendant announced our final approach into Dallas. The window-seat guy woke up. I looked out over the city. The Dallas area had a lot more water around it than I had expected. And brown haze.

"A lot of pollution down there," I commented to no one in particular.

"The air has gotten terrible here," the window guy responded.

The man in front of me straightened his seat, allowing my legs to move again. His son had disappeared back behind his seat. I glanced over to the man on my left.

"I enjoyed talking," I said. "You gave me some food for thought."

He smiled. "I'm glad. I enjoyed our conversation too."

The plane landed and started taxiing to its gate. I sensed the window guy leaning my way.

"You know," he said to both of us, "I overheard some of what you were saying about religion."

That's a shocker.

He continued. "I agree with some of what you said—the stupid stuff about religion. I mean, I go to movies, although not R-rated ones...well, except for *Saving Private Ryan,* which was great, and wasn't *The Passion of the Christ* rated R?"

The aisle guy answered for us. "Yes, it was."

"That was the bloodiest thing I ever saw. Have you ever seen so much blood?"

Neither of us responded.

"Anyway, people can get a little carried away with religious rules, but"—he was looking at the man on my left—"I think you're wrong when you say that religion stops people from enjoying life. In my experience, genuinely religious people—Christians, I mean—can enjoy life the most."

He looked back at me. "I'm not trying to be pushy. I simply think the two of you should consider that."

The plane stopped, everyone jumped out of their seats, and the noise level rose, effectively ending the conversation. *Hallelujah.*

Still seated, the man by the aisle leaned over and, in a half whisper, said, "He means well."

"I doubt that," I responded.

We remained in our seats as everyone around us stood with the personal items they had rushed to retrieve. *Why do people always do that? It's not like they can go anywhere.* The plane finally cleared back to us. The aisle guy rose and stepped away from his seat. He didn't seem to have any belongings. He grabbed a suitcase from an overhead bin and set it down behind him.

"Isn't this yours?" he asked me.

"Thanks."

I took my suitcase and stepped into the aisle. As I was extending the handle, I heard him say, "Until next time." I looked as he turned and walked toward the exit.

"Yeah," I said, wondering what he meant.

It took a second for me to get my bag situated on top of my suitcase. I pulled it down the aisle, through the jet bridge, and into the terminal. I scanned left and right but couldn't see the guy in either direction. *Why am I even looking for him?*

I started walking toward my connecting gate. I passed all the airport staples: newsstands, gift shops, bookstores, food places. I popped into a bookstore. In the "Top 20 Bestsellers" area, I couldn't help noticing six religious books. I glanced around—*Who am I afraid is going to see me?*—before picking up one and leafing through it. I put it down and read the back cover of another. I returned it to the rack. *What are these things really going to tell me?*

I ambled over to the paperback fiction section and got a copy of Nicholas Sparks's latest novel (I had adored his book *A Walk to Remember*). I pulled my suitcase over to the cash register and placed my book on the counter.

"Just this, please."

The cashier placed the book inside a store bag and rang me up. I grabbed it and my own bag and balanced them atop my suitcase. I continued down the terminal and across a long walkway into the next. Just about the time I saw my gate in the distance, I passed a Starbucks. *Exactly what I want.* I had more than an hour until takeoff—plenty of time for a latte. I entered the Starbucks and got in line behind two men. The first ordered a Frappuccino. The second requested the coffee of the day and some coffeecake. The voice sounded familiar. He paid, then turned around. It was the aisle guy.

"Hi," he said.

"Hi," I replied. "Fancy meeting you here."

The cashier gave him his items, then motioned toward me. I stepped forward slightly. "Nonfat grande vanilla latte, please. Decaf." I was dying for the caffeine, but I wanted to be good. "And an apple-cinnamon scone." I handed her a ten.

I turned to the man from the plane. "You have a layover?"

"Yes. How about you?"

"Just over an hour left."

She gave me my scone, and we slowly moved toward the serving island. The employee making the drinks placed one at the hand-off point. "Nonfat decaf grande vanilla latte," he said. I reached for it.

The aisle guy grabbed a couple of napkins. "Care to join me at a table?"

"Sure."

He headed for the sole empty one, near the entrance. We sat and sampled our coffees. It felt a little awkward, accepting this invitation. I was still married, after all. *But what's the harm in having coffee with some guy I met on a plane? I won't see him again. And it's not like I was looking for him...exactly. Besides, he is a counselor.*

"So," he asked, "did you buy something at the bookstore?"

"How did you know I stopped at the bookstore?" I responded suspiciously.

"The bag you are carrying."

"Oh." I glanced over at it. "Yeah. I did. Nicholas Sparks. I've been wanting something good to read."

I took a bite of scone, then washed it down with some of my latte. A question was forming in my mind. Given our previous conversation, I knew how he would answer. But I wanted to talk it through with someone, and this guy seemed safe, in more ways than one. And I valued his opinion. So…

"I was wondering…"

"Yes?"

"I was wondering, and I feel kind of stupid asking this, because of what we were talking about before…"

"Sincere questions aren't stupid."

"Well…" I couldn't make it sound any different than it did. "Do you think it's possible for someone to connect personally with God?"

six

It was the last question I ever expected to hear myself ask. I didn't even know if God existed. Now here I was asking this guy about personally connecting with God. He seemed to take it entirely in stride, however. Which is what I wanted, actually—someone with whom I could safely explore possibilities.

"Why do you ask?" he responded.

"Well," I answered, "given what we said before, about religion, you're probably going to think this is the dumbest thing you've ever heard. But after we talked, I started thinking about what's been happening with Nick. Him and his religious stuff, I mean. And as I thought about it, it still didn't make any sense to me. It doesn't at all fit who Nick is or what he would normally do. And, I don't know. I just got to thinking, maybe...maybe Nick really did have an encounter with God. Or Jesus. Or something." I paused for a second. "I know—that sounds pretty far-fetched."

"No, not really."

"But you don't even believe in God," I said.

"Your husband does, and he is the one focused on connecting with God. It seems to me, then, that it's worth your exploring."

I was surprised by his answer, but I was glad to have someone willing to talk it through. At least, I thought he was offering to talk about it.

"So do you think it's possible?" I asked. "Someone actually connecting with God?"

"What do you think?"

"Well, since I'm not sure there even is a God..."

"Are you saying that you don't believe in God or that you just don't know what to think about the possibility of God?"

I thought about that for a second. "I just don't know what to think about it, I guess."

"Then you think it's possible there is a God?"

"Well...it's possible, I suppose. I know, you probably think that's crazy."

"Why don't we assume that there is and go from there? Maybe we can figure out something about what Nick's going through."

That seemed like a reasonable way to explore the topic and maybe to discover some answers.

"Okay," I replied. "That seems good."

"So what if God does exist? Do you think it would be possible to connect with him?"

I answered honestly. "No, not really. I mean, God would be so much bigger and more powerful—so far beyond us, I guess—that I don't think we could presume to connect with him. What would be the basis for the connection? It would be like an ant trying to connect with us."

"That's a good question." He sipped his coffee. "What if you looked at it from the other side?"

"How do you mean?"

"I mean from God's viewpoint."

"What—could God relate to us?"

"No. Rather, would he want to?"

I considered that for a moment. "It's the same. I think the answer's the same. If there is a God, and he, or she, or whatever, is big enough to create the whole universe and all the time that's involved, billions of years, and here we are stuck out on this little planet in this nondescript galaxy—Nick always loves telling me about this astronomy stuff—anyway, what possible need would God have for us?"

"That's an extremely good question."

"I just have a hard time believing that any God would have much use for people, much less want to connect with them. I mean, wouldn't he have more important things to do?"

He laughed. "You might think that." He took a bite of his coffeecake and wiped his mouth with his napkin. "Maybe the answer to that question would lie in the nature of God."

"Meaning…"

"What would God be like? Would he just create everything, let it go, and watch it from a distance? Or, even further disconnected, would God be an impersonal force, like in *Star Wars*? Or would God be an involved being who thinks, chooses, and feels—who loves—like we do?"

I finished a sip of my latte. "Who knows? It's not like God makes a grand appearance to everyone. Who knows what God would be like?"

"Well"—he took a long drink—"work from the evidence you have. If there is a God, don't you think there would be clues as to what he is like?"

"Clues?" The cover of *The Da Vinci Code* suddenly popped into my brain. "What kind of clues?"

"What the universe would say about its Creator."

"Well, he'd have to be really old." I laughed.

"What?" he asked, grinning with me.

"I'm just picturing some really old guy who's kind of shriveled up and doesn't move around too well anymore, like they make actors look old in movies. God wouldn't be like that, I suppose. If you've been around for billions of years, you don't age, exactly."

He smiled. "No, I wouldn't think so." He had another sip of coffee. "So God would be really old. What else?"

"He'd have to be really smart. The universe is pretty intricate. And humans themselves are so complex, given what we've learned about DNA and all."

"Okay, God would have to be superintelligent."

"Yeah. I'm not sure I buy that design in the universe proves God, but if there was a God, he would be really intelligent—and powerful—to pull it all off."

"Why is that?"

"If we all got here by the Big Bang, then God would have had to fine-tune it to make the universe we have. I've heard Nick talk about how precise the whole thing is, how if just one of a thousand things were a little out of balance, the whole universe would be different, or we wouldn't be here at all."

I'm starting to sound like an advocate for the existence of God. But we are presuming that God exists...

"Okay," he said. "So if God exists, he would be really old, superintelligent, and very powerful—at least as powerful as the universe itself?"

"If he put it all into motion, then, yeah, I would say so."

"It sounds as though you're saying that whatever traits the creation has would reflect some greater trait in the Creator—age, intelligence, power."

I decided to think about that one for a minute. I didn't want anyone putting words into my mouth. I broke off a piece of my scone.

Could what he just said be true? Would the universe reflect the Creator? I suppose that's kind of a given. Whatever we make reflects us. Like my graphics. How could it be otherwise? What we create can only come out of who we are.

"All right," I answered. "That's a fair summary. I'm not saying I think it proves God."

"Understood." He had a bite of coffeecake. "So what if we bring this down to the level of people?"

"I'm not sure I'm following you."

"People are part of the universe. The highest native intelligence on earth. What would people tell us about God?"

"What do you think?" I asked. "I've been doing all the thinking here."

He laughed. "Okay, fine. I'll think a little too. I think that the various aspects of our being—our mind, our emotions, our capacity to choose, our conscience—would all reflect God. In other words, humanity's traits, just like the universe, would reflect the Creator. And the highest form of creation would most closely resemble who God is."

"Meaning people."

"Yes."

"But people can be awful to each other. You're not saying that's who God is too, are you?"

"That's a hard question, isn't it?" He sipped his coffee again. "Because evil exists. Is that part of who God would be, or instead has something gone wrong?"

"I don't know. If God was part evil, that would be pretty bleak. All I know is, the world is really screwed up, and lately it seems to be getting worse, not better. It's a little frightening to have children and not know when the next bomb will go off or something."

"I know," he replied. "It is frightening."

He had another piece of his coffeecake, and I had some more scone.

"You mentioned your daughter—Sara?"

"Yeah."

"Do you have a picture?"

"Of course."

I pulled my billfold out of my bag and held out Sara's picture to him. It was a really good one, with her new blue dress against a backdrop of red and yellow tulips at the arboretum. She had a pigtail sprouting out of each side of her head, and she did look precious.

"She's adorable," he commented.

"Thanks. We think so." I couldn't help smiling at the picture one last time before returning it to my bag.

"What do you do with her when you're working?" he asked.

"I take her to my cousin's three days a week. She has a three-year-old and a fourteen-month-old. Sara does great with them."

"How do you do being away from her like that?"

"I do okay. I really like my work, and I'm not sure how I'd do without a break from parenting sometimes. But some days I do have mixed feelings."

"Why is that?"

"It's just that when they're little, they do things every day that mean the world. Yesterday I had Sara at home, and we were talking about going to visit her grandmother and how Grandma was my mommy. Of course, she doesn't really understand how all that works yet, but she looked at me with those big round eyes and said, 'Mommy, I like you to be my mommy.' It just melts your heart."

He smiled broadly. "I bet it does."

I pointed a finger at him jokingly. "You just wait. One day if you have a little girl, she'll look at you like that, and you'll want to give her anything she asks for. It's worse for dads, I think. Nick would give Sara the world."

"Tell me," he said. "What do you like best about being a mom?"

I could feel a big grin slide over my face, and a joy washed over me just thinking about it. "Everything. You treasure the time they sit on your lap…feeling their soft hair, taking in their unique scent, being warmed by their little legs and back on you. Your own child is truly the most beautiful child in the world. You study her features more closely than any other person does. She comes from you, and she resembles you. You touch and hold her more than anyone else does, so you're able to absorb all there is about her in a unique way."

A smile had grown on his face as I spoke. "What else?"

"You love it when they discover something, like conquering the stairs or waving bye-bye. You love bragging about them to anyone. You could fill a book with how much you love them, how wonderful they are, and how they learn new things day after day."

I paused for a second, thinking about the things I treasured most about Sara and how I would go through all that again. "You know what else you love? You love the sound of their voice above all other kids'. It feels wonderful when Sara finds me and runs to me in a crowd of other kids and parents."

I thought about that morning at the breakfast table. "Though you can't always, you really want to give them what they want, like the sugary cereal or a stuffed animal—even if Sara already has more than I can count. You delight in the happiness it brings them, even if it's fleeting. And when they're naughty—which is often enough—you sometimes have to hold back your smile because they are so precious to you. Maybe that's what I like best: loving someone so much, regardless of what they do."

He leaned forward, put his elbows on the table, and intertwined his fingers. "Let me ask you this. If there was a God who created everything, don't you think it's possible that he would feel the same way about you that you feel about Sara? Love you as much? Want to give you the world? Want to be as connected to you as you are to her? In other words, is it possible that your love for Sara is a reflection of who the Creator is?"

I leaned away from the table and thought for a moment. "I don't know," I answered honestly. "I've never really considered that before."

He continued. "Do you think that people's desire to connect with God could have come from him? That God might have placed within them the desire for such a connection, because he is the one who actually wants it? That he designed them for intimacy with himself, and they are incomplete without it?"

"Maybe. I suppose it's possible."

"If this was the case, would Nick's course be a reasonable response to that God-placed desire? Would Nick's wanting a close connection with God be nonsense, or would it make the most sense?"

I sensed that we weren't dealing in hypotheticals any longer.

seven

"YOU SOUND LIKE you actually believe in God," I said tensely.

"I do."

"But...you said you didn't."

"Not at all. I said I hate religion."

"What's the difference?"

"Religion is what people mistakenly do to try to get to God—by being good enough, keeping certain rules, performing certain rituals, and so forth. But God? Of course I believe in him."

This was completely not what I was expecting.

"So you also think it's possible to know God personally?"

"Yes. I know it is."

I could feel my blood pressure rising. *This has all been a setup. He has the same agenda as Mr. Evangelism on the first flight, whose approach didn't work. So he pretended to be on my side. And I fell for the whole thing!*

"You're no better than that guy on the plane—no, worse! Here I am, pouring my heart out to you about my marriage, and all you want is to trap me into talking about God. At least the other guy was straightforward in his approach."

I reached for my latte and my bag.

"I wasn't trying to trick you," he replied. "I was simply helping you do what you said you wanted—to explore why Nick might be on this new course. I couldn't do that by stating up front my own perspective. You were too closed for that. But thinking through the issues and reaching your own conclusions—that's what you're trying to do, isn't it?"

Oh. Yeah. I am trying to do that, aren't I?

I folded my arms across my chest. "Okay," I conceded, "maybe I did say that."

I let myself calm down just a little. *But I'm still not happy with the subterfuge. Or with where this guy is coming from.*

I decided to give his motivation the benefit of the doubt and keep on conversing. *It's not that long before my next plane, so I won't have to endure much more if I get sick of it. And despite his religious beliefs, he is a counselor. Maybe he can actu-*

ally help. After all, how many counselors are willing to offer free advice during a trip?

I steered us back to my specific situation—Nick. "But not everyone's spiritual pursuit involves becoming so zealous as to claim to dine with Jesus. I mean, have you ever heard anyone say that?"

"It's been a while, I admit."

"Surely you're not saying that you think Nick really dined with Jesus."

"I think only you can decide whether to believe his story or not. I'm just trying to help you assess whether his direction of connecting with God is a reasonable one."

"And you think it is."

"Certainly. But I can't make up your mind for you. And I'm not the one who has to live your marriage."

"That's the truth." *Be thankful.*

I took another drink of my latte. "You said something a minute ago. You said that if God designed people for an intimate connection with himself, then we are incomplete without him. But don't you think that God is just a crutch for some people?"

"I suppose that depends on what you were created for," he answered. "If you were created for life without God, then he's a crutch. If, on the other hand, the very reason you were created is for an intimate relationship with God, then he's not a crutch. He's the fulfillment of what you were created to be."

"But you're implying that people can only be fulfilled through an intimate connection with God."

"Yes."

"But that's not true."

"Do you think people are truly satisfied in other things?"

"Of course. There are lots of people who are fulfilled who don't have God in their lives."

"Are you?"

"Well, no. But I'm not everybody."

"You are more everybody than you realize."

"I feel fulfilled in my career, for the most part."

"And as a parent," he added.

"Definitely as a parent."

"But not as a wife."

I could feel my eyes give a slight roll. "No. That doesn't rank quite as high on the fulfillment scale."

"Why not, do you think?"

"I don't know. I suppose I had this fantasy of what marriage would be like, starting with the wedding. Doesn't every woman have that? Well, we didn't make it through the ceremony without that fantasy going awry. I should have known we were in trouble when the minister, instead of saying that the rings represented an endless circle of love, said they represented an endless circus of love. It was his second wedding, and he was dyslexic, we were later told. I don't even know why we got married in a church. Anyway, he was right, after all."

"A lot of people start off on the wrong foot."

"Yeah, well, we never got on the right one. At least that's how it felt. That wasn't the case before we got married. Things were great then. But things are always great at the beginning of relationships. It's later I get bored. Except with Nick I really didn't. I stayed interested in him."

A large flight or two must have deplaned, because suddenly the ordering line had almost backed up to our table. We both shifted our chairs around to give people more room to stand, then picked up where we left off.

"What kept you interested in Nick, do you think?"

"I think it was because his whole world didn't revolve around me. He was real focused on his career, and I liked that."

"You don't seem to like it anymore."

"That's the truth. I suppose I got exactly what I wanted—someone who had another life, who wasn't too clingy. Now it's not enough."

"What would you say you want out of marriage?"

"I guess I want to be intimate in a way that's just as satisfying as the passion we first had. I know you can't sustain that level of passion forever; no one can. But I thought it would be replaced by an emotional closeness that would be just as good, in a sense. That hasn't happened, though."

I took a final sip of my latte, then continued. "Have you ever felt that way—a fulfilling emotional connection in a long-lasting relationship?"

"Yes, I feel that way all the time."

"You do?" I was taken aback by his answer. "How?"

"Well." He smiled. "That's kind of an involved story."

I glanced at my watch. *If we have time, I would kind of like to know his secret.*

He resumed. "What do you think stops you from experiencing that in your marriage?"

I pondered that for a moment. "I just don't feel completely known by Nick. He thinks he knows me, but he doesn't really understand what makes me tick, what my dreams really are, what… I don't know. For the longest time it was his work that kept him distant. And now, I suppose, it's this Jesus thing."

I felt myself straighten in my chair. "I do not plan on

being married to someone who lies in bed next to me watching a guy on TV touching people's foreheads, and then they fall down and pretend to be healed. I mean, who could stand that?"

He chuckled. "Is that what Nick watches?"

"No. Not yet. Or maybe he sneaks it in while I'm in the bathroom."

He laughed a little louder. I did too at the image of Nick flipping to those religious networks while I was brushing my teeth, as if they were the Playboy channel or something.

"So what if your marriage were more fulfilling?" he asked. "Would that satisfy you?"

"It would help."

"But would the deepest part of you be filled?"

"I don't know. It's just hard to imagine that with Nick."

"Would it have mattered if it had been someone else?"

"Well...maybe."

"Like who?"

"Like..." Only one person ever came to mind when I thought about this. "There was this guy I dated for a year in high school, Jason Payne. I was so head over heels about him. And ever since, I've wondered what might have happened if we had stayed together."

The ordering line had receded back to the counter. Nevertheless, I lowered my voice a little. "I think about him pretty often, actually. That sounds terrible, I know."

"It simply sounds like someone who isn't fulfilled. So what happened to the relationship?"

"He was a year ahead of me, and he was going to Stanford for college, and I started getting cold feet. I was afraid that he was going to meet someone there and that we wouldn't last, because I was going to stay in the Midwest for school. I didn't want to risk that rejection, and he had done a couple of things that annoyed me, so before he left, I broke up with him. It was the stupidest thing I ever did."

"You think you would have been happier with him?"

"Well..." I didn't like the sound of the truth. "Yeah. I do think that. That's not to say that I don't love Nick. Or didn't, anyway."

He leaned forward in his chair. "You know, you wouldn't have been any more fulfilled with Jason."

"How do you know?" *That's a pretty bold statement to make.*

"Because I know Jason."

"You do? Jason Payne? From Evanston? How do you know him?" I was trying to keep the excitement out of my voice.

"He met me after he moved to the Silicon Valley area. He's still there."

"Doing what? Is he married?" That sounded truly pathetic.

"He was. Twice."

"Twice? He's already been married two times?"

"Yes."

"What happened?"

"Both of them left him."

"They left *him*? Why would anyone do that?"

"Let's just say that he had his own issues. With which, I am happy to say, he is doing much better."

"Did you meet him professionally? I mean, in your counseling?"

"Not exactly. More of a personal relationship."

I sat back and stared forward. I couldn't believe it. Here I had entertained this fantasy for all these years: what if I hadn't broken up with Jason? And now, in the course of two minutes, that fantasy had been dashed to pieces.

"And, no," he said, "being with you instead wouldn't have helped him. He needed something more than a loving wife."

I hate how counselors sometimes know just what you are thinking.

"And marrying Jason," he added, "even with his having

worked through some of his issues, wouldn't have ultimately satisfied you, either."

"And why not?" *Dashing my fantasy is bad enough. You don't have to keep stomping on it.*

"Because people's souls are never filled up by human relationships. There is the initial thrill of romance and the chemical high that accompanies it, all of which is great. But that wears off. Eventually people settle into a relationship and find that it can't meet their heart's deepest longings. It wasn't meant to, so it's no surprise, really, that it doesn't."

"You're not saying that relationships are unimportant."

"No, not at all," he responded. "I'm just saying that true fulfillment can't be found in the created realm. Only God himself can satisfy the human heart. You were created for God. Nothing else will satisfy."

"But I don't believe that. I see happy people around all the time."

"How well do you truly know them, though? They may all be just like you: they have meaningful aspects of their lives, but ultimately they are not fulfilled. It's not that hard to put on a good face when you're around others."

"I just think lots of people are fulfilled—in their work, in relationships, in causes they devote themselves to. Plenty of things."

He looked at me for a moment. "Do you really think that? I don't think you do. Look at the society you live in. The list of things people try to fill themselves with is endless—alcohol, drugs, food, work, television, video games, sports, sex, shopping. I could go on. But nothing on this planet will satisfy the human soul."

"But not everyone is addicted or compulsive," I objected.

"No, some aren't. They seek fulfillment through parenting, balanced work, exercise, healthy relationships, social service. There are many positive things to devote yourself to. But these still don't fill the heart. When people get to the end of their lives—even those who have had good careers or marriages or parenting experiences—they're still not ultimately satisfied."

"How do you know?"

"Well, for one, many of them tell me. They won't tell anyone else, but when no one else is listening, they tell me."

"Why—because you're a counselor?"

"I suppose that has something to do with it."

"And what do they say?"

"That what they experienced wasn't enough. It may have been a good life, but deep down there is still some emptiness in their hearts."

"And you think that's because..."

"Because how is your heart going to be filled by someone, or something, as finite and imperfect as you are? If people were created to have an intimate connection with their Creator, would you expect them to be satisfied apart from him?"

He wiped his mouth with his napkin and set it on his pastry bag. "Maybe Nick has come to realize that, as important as you and Sara are to him—and I have no doubt you are—his heart was made for something more, for something transcendent, and he couldn't be fulfilled without it.

"And," he continued, "you're searching for something deeper too. Even if you don't know it yet."

"I'm just hoping for things to get a little better."

"That's the problem. Things don't usually get any better. Circumstantially, life is what it is. People hope things will improve, but they rarely do. Tomorrow will have its own set of frustrations and stresses and disappointments. Or things may get worse. You could lose your career. Or your family. Or your friends. Or your health."

"Sure," I replied, "those things could happen. But I can't base my life on that possibility."

He raised his eyebrows. "Possibility? Most of those things will happen. To everyone. There's only one thing that can't be taken away from you. When you find your fulfillment there, you can't ever lose it."

He unexpectedly stood up and pushed his seat under the table.

"We'd better go," he said.

"Why?"

"Our flight is boarding."

"Our?"

"You're going to Tucson, aren't you?"

eight

"BUT THE FLIGHT DOESN'T BOARD for another twenty minutes," I objected, looking at my watch.

"It's boarding now. Trust me."

"How do you know?"

"I just know. Can I carry your suitcase?"

I got up and placed my bag above my rolling suitcase. "No, I've got it."

We walked down to the gate, and, sure enough, they were calling my group. I got out my boarding pass and glanced at it. *An F seat. Next to the window. At least I'm not in the middle.*

The plane actually didn't look quite as crowded as the last one. Almost all the middle seats remained vacant as I walked down the plane to my row. I stopped. The counselor waited behind me while I put my suitcase overhead. I slid across two empty seats and got into mine before turning back to say farewell.

"Well, you've given me some food for thought," I said. "It was certainly an interesting conversation. What row are you on?"

"This one," he said as he sat down in the aisle seat on my row.

"This one?" I grabbed the boarding pass out of his hand and looked at it. *My row. Seat D.*

I handed it back to him. "Sorry. I was just surprised that we are on the same row again." He took the boarding pass and slipped it into his shirt pocket.

"Don't you think it's a strange coincidence," I asked, "our being next to each other two flights in a row?"

"No. Not really."

I put my bag in the seat between us. It didn't look like anyone would be sitting there. And it provided a kind of buffer in case the conversation took a turn I didn't want. Which it already had, I suppose. Here we were, talking about fulfillment in life and God and so forth, but somehow, with this man, I was more drawn in than turned off.

I was curious as to where he was heading right before we left Starbucks. But it did seem a little awkward, our getting on an entirely new flight, two strangers sitting next to each other again. And discussing the meaning of life. I thought maybe it was a good time to back up for a moment and at least get officially acquainted.

"I never did introduce myself," I said. "I'm Mattie." I reached across myself with my right hand.

He awkwardly bent his own hand around his armrest and shook mine. "Hi, Mattie. Call me Jay."

"Good to meet you, finally."

"You too," he said, smiling.

"Why are you headed to Tucson?" I asked.

"Business."

"What kind of business?"

"My father and I run a management operation, so to speak."

"Management of what?"

"Pretty much everything."

This guy is not real big on specifics.

"I thought you were a counselor."

"I am."

"You do that on the side?"

"No, it's part of the same operation."

I couldn't imagine what kind of operation that was, exactly, but I let it drop.

The plane's engines revved up. I looked out the window as we sped down the runway and took off. Once we were above the clouds, I turned back toward Jay. I figured we would resume our conversation where we had left off, but he had put his tray table down and was writing on a pad of paper. *Where did that come from? I didn't see him carrying anything.*

I watched him for a couple of moments, but he didn't look up. I decided to read my new book. It started quickly, as all Sparks's novels do.

The flight attendants arrived with drinks. I got another cranapple juice, which Jay handed to me. He got some water. And we both got the ubiquitous pretzels.

I opened mine—*Here I go, some more useless calories from a food I don't even like*—as he set his pretzels on the middle seat.

He started writing again. I opened my book and resumed reading. After a minute I set the book down and leaned slightly toward him. "What are you writing?"

"Oh, some favorite words of mine."

"Like what?"

"Poetry, mostly."

"Poetry?" I laughed a little. "You didn't say you were a poet."

"Someone else wrote it, actually."

"What are you trying to do, impress me?" I said half joking.

He smiled but didn't reply. To be honest, I was already impressed. I'd never met anybody quite like him.

"May I see some of it?"

He handed the pad to me. "It's free verse. At least it is in English."

I started reading.

I have loved you with a love that never ends.
Though the mountains be shaken
And the hills be removed,
Yet my unfailing love for you will not be shaken.

How could I give you up?
My heart is turned over within me.
I will take great delight in you,
I will quiet you with my love,
I will rejoice over you with singing.

"This is really good," I commented. "I mean, I love the intensity of feeling. Who wrote it?"

"My father did."

"You're kidding. What was the story behind it? What inspired him?"

"A relationship he had. One that he desperately wanted back."

I handed him his pad. He set it on the middle seat and opened his pretzels.

"God wants to love you with this kind of love," he said. "A passionate love."

"Passionate?" That was the last word I would have applied to God.

"God is pursuing you. He wants you to be connected with him forever."

I sipped my juice. "But I don't feel loved by God. Much less pursued by him."

"That's because you're so deadened to his voice. Everyone is at first. Humanity rejected God, and it's been deaf to him ever since."

"But that's too easy. To say we're all deaf to God—to me that just means God doesn't exist. If I say, 'Prove God to me,' and you say, 'Well, you're deaf to him; if you weren't, you'd hear him,' that's too convenient. It's just taking the facts and making up a story that fits them."

"Oh, people aren't entirely deaf to God," he replied. "They hear his voice in a variety of ways—just not nearly as clearly as they could if they were connected to him. It's like the difference between my listening to you and my listening to the captain when he came on a few minutes ago to tell us something about the flight, which was all garbled. Could you make out much of what he was saying?"

"No."

"People are like that toward God. They can hear him a little, but they can't make out much of what he's saying. When Sara was born and you held her in your arms and looked at her for the first time and you couldn't believe you could love anything so much, that was God speaking."

"That's exactly how I felt. I couldn't believe how much I could love this little person."

"When you stand above the California coast and look out to the Pacific Ocean, you feel so small. You know there has to be something greater than yourself in the world."

"I've experienced that."

"That's God speaking. When you fail to love Nick, and instead are angry and bitter and you retaliate, your guilt is God speaking through your conscience. You know that you weren't meant to live that way. It seems less than you were created to be, doesn't it?"

I shifted in my seat and looked out the window for a moment. I felt a tug toward what he was saying and a tug away from it. I turned back toward him. "Yeah, maybe. But it's almost impossible not to be resentful."

"I know it is. I'm just talking here about God speaking to your heart. All these things touch something deep within you because you were made for intimacy with God. He is the something bigger, the one who loves more than you could imagine, the one who forgives instead of being bitter. Connecting with him deeply is what your heart longs for. There is no being as delightful as he is."

Delightful? God? Delightful? I would have placed him more on the boring side of the spectrum.

As if reading my thoughts, he continued. "God is the least boring, the most fascinating, sublime, enchanting being that exists. How could he be otherwise? Delighting in God simply means that you derive your greatest joy and pleasure from him, because of who he is."

"Pleasure from God? You've got to be kidding."

"No, not in the least."

"How could anyone find pleasure in God? I mean, I can understand believing in God, but—"

"That's the statement of someone who's cut off from God. You don't realize how upside down what you just said is."

"What's that supposed to mean?" I replied somewhat defensively.

He had a drink of water and thought for a moment. "You know the hypothetical question, who would you want to have dinner with if you could dine with anyone from history?"

"Sure. I guess."

"What if you could dine with the one who carved the Grand Canyon, raised the Rocky Mountains, coded DNA, invented nuclear fusion, designed language, created the stars, establishes justice, fashions every newborn, and loves without end?"

"But God doesn't drop in on people for dinner."

He smiled. "Well, maybe. But what I am saying is this: God far surpasses any person or thing or experience this world could possibly offer. God is infinitely more delightful than anything or anyone he has made."

"But God—I mean, even if there is a God—reaching out to him… Who would know where to start?"

"You don't have to start," he answered. "God has already started. He is already reaching out to you. That's why he became a person."

"You know, if I could actually have dinner with Jesus, like Nick allegedly did, maybe I could believe too."

"Faith is a lot easier than you think. And you don't really need Jesus to show up. You do need to let go of what keeps you from trusting him and connecting with him."

"What's that?"

"You tell me."

I turned away and stared blankly out the window again. A swell of anger grew within me. I turned back his way and spoke measuredly, trying to keep my voice low enough so no one else would hear.

"Okay, I'll tell you what would keep me from trusting God and even wanting to connect with him. My younger sister was abused—sexually abused—by our uncle for six years, starting at age eight. I didn't even know for several years."

I paused to make sure I retained my composure. "Her life was ruined. And I couldn't stop it. I tried to, but I couldn't stop it."

I looked him straight in the eye. "I couldn't trust any God who would let that happen to her."

nine

HE RESPONDED slowly and quietly. "What you and your sister have endured is horrible. God hates it, just as you do. But how much of the world's evil would you like him to stop?"

"All of it!" I felt tears welling up in my eyes. "All of it! Can't he do that?"

"Yes, he could."

"Then why doesn't he?" I felt the first tears trickle down my cheeks. *Oh, great. I'm starting to blubber.* "I mean, look at my sister. Look at what that did to her. She starts sleeping around when she's in junior high. She gets pregnant. She drops out of school. She never trusts men. She's had two failed marriages with absolute jerks. She can't hold a decent job, she drinks too much, and she keeps looking for I-don't-know-what in these guys she takes home. Are you saying this was God's plan for her?"

I fumbled in my bag for a Kleenex, dabbed my eyes, then looked up at him. I saw something I never expected to see. His eyes were tearing up too.

"No," he said softly. "No. That is not God's ultimate plan for her. And it breaks my heart that she has had to go through all that. It breaks the Father's heart too."

Seeing his tears made mine return. "Then why didn't God stop it?"

"Mattie, there are no words I could say that would make sense, no reasons that would take away your pain. But I can tell you this. God is at work restoring people to their original design: to be connected to him, to be in a love relationship with him by their own choosing. One day the evil will be done away with, and all that will be left is good."

"But what about the people who do such evil in this world?"

"All things will be accounted for. The victims will be avenged, the perpetrators punished, the evil eradicated, the good rewarded. It's living during this not-yet time that's the tough part—knowing how terrible things are sometimes and how good they ought to be."

"I just don't understand why we have to wait."

"When humanity turned its back on God, it plunged itself into a world of great evil. Because of his love for people, God is at work making them into what he intended them to be. But he doesn't force them. That's the only way love can work. You have to choose to receive love, and you have to choose to give love. If you don't choose freely, it's not love."

"So is that it?" I asked, dabbing my eyes once more. "Are we just resigned to living with all this?"

"Recovering what humanity lost is a slow, person-by-person process. The human heart, once distanced from God, is not easily won back to its source of life and goodness. It seems like it would be, but it isn't."

"It just doesn't seem fair. My sister didn't ask to be abused."

"No, she didn't. It wasn't fair. It was horrible. God knows how horrible it was."

"I doubt that. I really doubt that. How could he know, sitting up there, or wherever, just watching?"

An expression of genuine hurt came over his face. "Is that what you think God does? Distance himself from the pain of people?"

"That's what it seems like."

"Humanity's rejection of God was incredibly painful for him. He had to watch his own children fall into darkness.

Can you imagine what it would be like to watch Sara's life spiral downward due to drugs?"

That image made me cringe on the inside. "Okay. So it was hard for God to watch us. But he doesn't do anything about it."

He shook his head. "No, you're wrong. He did the most that could be done. That guy on the first plane, the one talking to you about God—remember him?"

"How could I forget?"

"He didn't know you, so he didn't have the most sensitive approach—"

"You can say that again."

"But he did have some things right. He was right about the incredible suffering that God endured at the hands of humanity in his effort to win them back. You saw *The Passion of the Christ.*"

"Which I regretted."

"The violence that Jesus endured only makes sense if you understand that here was God taking upon himself the punishment for the sins of humanity. He would do anything to be reconnected with those he loves—even die for them."

"Even if Jesus was God dying for humanity, what good did it do? Everything is still so screwed up on this planet. I mean, it's been two thousand years."

"What Jesus did was open a way back to God. He provided forgiveness—a clean slate—and the opportunity for people to be connected with God."

"But then what do you do? Once someone has connected with God, do they just sit around saying, 'Hey, now I'm connected to God!'?"

He laughed. "No. Not at all. Once you and God are joined to each other, you do what you do in any relationship: converse with him, get to know him, learn to delight in him."

"You mean you pray?"

"Yes. Although that word may not describe it well for you."

"But anyone can pray to God."

"Yes, but not everyone can hear him talk back. That's what a true relationship is all about. It's about deeply communing with another person. Once you establish a connection with God, he will teach you."

"Teach me what?"

"To listen."

"Do you think that's what Nick is doing?" I asked. "Learning to listen?"

"It's part of what he's doing—a crucial part."

"But what exactly does that involve—other than reading the Bible, which Nick has been doing lately. Anyone can do that."

"Yes, but not everyone can hear God speaking to them through it like Nick now can."

I was taken aback by his statement. "What? What makes Nick so special?" *He is my husband, and he is talented, but he doesn't seem that extraordinary to me.*

"What makes Nick so special is that he is no longer the person he used to be. God has given him a new spirit."

"But what's the difference between that and just becoming religious? It's the same thing."

A baby was crying a number of rows back. I turned that direction. It might have been crying for a while; I'd been pretty wrapped up in our conversation. Three years before, the sound would have driven me crazy, but with a two-year-old of my own now, I had a lot more patience. The mother stood up and walked the baby toward the rear of the plane. I turned back to Jay.

He resumed. "It's not the same thing at all. Just the opposite. Becoming religious is about outward things mostly. Do this. Don't do that. Go here. Avoid going there. I'm talking about someone becoming new from the inside out. When you put your trust in Jesus, God gives you a brand-new spirit, a clean one."

"You mean, like a new attitude?"

"No, an actual new human spirit. The old one was dead

to God. It couldn't connect with him. You have to have a new one, one that's alive to God. He then comes to live in you, and he connects with you on the deepest possible level—a level where you can hear him."

"So you're saying Nick is experiencing this now?"

"Yes."

"What does that mean exactly? Nick isn't hearing an audible voice from God, is he?"

"No, of course not. He doesn't need to. God's Spirit can communicate directly with Nick. Usually the Spirit does that through God's written word."

"The Bible?"

"Yes."

"So what if someone does establish this connection with God? What does God have to say to them?"

"The things I wrote before, for one."

"The poetry? I thought you said your father wrote that."

"God is my father."

That sounded a little strange, but I let it pass. "Those things were from the Bible?" I asked.

"Yes."

"But I've always thought of the Bible as mostly a rule book…how to be a good person, you know."

"Then you've missed its message entirely."

He reached for his pen and wrote some more as I watched. When he finished, he handed the pad to me. "Does this sound like a rule book?"

I read what he had written.

Therefore I am now going to allure you;
I will lead you into the desert
And speak tenderly to you.

I have engraved you on the palms of my hands.
As the bridegroom rejoices over his bride,
So I rejoice over you.
Therefore my heart yearns for you.
One day, you will call me "my husband."
I will betroth you to me forever;
I will betroth you to me in love.

I have made myself one spirit with you.
I nourish you; I cherish you.
I give myself up for you.
I lay down my life for you.

I looked up at him. "The Bible says these things?"

"Yes. God wants to say them to you. He wants to say

them when you read his word. He wants to whisper them to you as you go through your day. When you stop to be quiet and listen, he wants to say these things, and so much more, to your heart. That's the way Jesus lived on earth. He listened to his father's voice."

"So are you saying that Christianity is just sitting around quietly and listening?"

"No, hardly. Life with the God who loves you is many things. Loving God and loving others, when you boil it down. But no one can do that adequately. Only God can. That's why he joins himself to people, to live his supernatural life through them. A life of love is simply the outflow of God through a person."

"And that comes through listening?"

"In large part. Your heart is changed by deeply knowing God's heart toward you. Hearing how you are loved. Hearing how you are forgiven. Hearing how you are accepted and delighted in and how you have a special place in God's family. What if you lived in a place where these were the constant messages you received?"

"That would be a nice place."

"And it's available to you now. You can find that place in Jesus Christ, through faith in him."

I thought about the messages that I did consume—

about needing to be the perfect mom, the perfect wife, the successful professional, the woman who could keep up with models who were always younger, prettier, skinnier. Who could measure up to all of it?

He continued. "What God wants to say to you is something you need to hear from him every day, just as Sara needs to hear from you and be shown every day that you love her."

I thought about Sara. Then for some reason my sister popped back into my mind. "What about Julie?" I asked somberly. "She hasn't experienced much of God's love."

"That doesn't mean God hasn't loved her. I can tell you this: in the midst of all her pain, your sister will choose to be reconnected with God. She will know his love deeply. And there will come a day when God will personally wipe away every tear from her eyes. She'll never hurt again. And the hurt she did experience here will seem as nothing to her then, for she will have God."

"But she's having to go through so much now. And I hurt so much for her."

"You know what? She hurts for you, the things you are having to go through. The issue isn't whether we've experienced pain. All people have, even those who seem to have it all together. God is bigger than people's pain, and he can heal it. God's love heals all."

I sat back, somewhat stunned. "This isn't at all what I understood Christianity to be."

"It's what you were designed for: to be joined to God, to know his love, to relate to him intimately."

I certainly didn't want to commit myself to anything, but I couldn't help but ask the logical question. "So what do I do with this?"

"You have to answer this: do you want to be joined to perfect love?"

ten

A FLIGHT ATTENDANT came on the overhead speaker and announced that we were starting our descent into Tucson. Jay put his tray table up. I noticed that he hadn't reclined his seat.

I sat quietly in my thoughts for a moment. *I can't believe what I'm considering. I got on this plane, avoiding God and ready to divorce Nick, and now… But do I have to go down this path to…*

I waited for Jay to turn to me before I spoke. "Are you implying that I have to go down the same path as Nick to save my marriage?"

"No."

"But it seems like it. Here Nick is going off in his own

direction, and I just feel like he's getting farther away from me."

"That depends on what you mean," he said. "Nick is getting farther away from trying to find fulfillment in life without God. So if that is your common ground, you're right."

That doesn't sound particularly hopeful.

He continued. "But in a very real sense, Nick is moving closer to you. He is growing in his ability to truly know you and truly love you. That's what you want in your marriage, isn't it—to be known and loved?"

"Yeah. That would be nice."

"And Nick is learning to do that better. Of course, he won't ever do it perfectly. He can't fill the deepest parts of your soul. Only God can."

Maybe so. But I still wish I had more of that from Nick. "You say Nick is changing, learning to love better. How—" *I don't know any way not to make this sound self-centered.* "How is that going to happen? Because I'm not going to feel all that loved if Nick just sits around all day reading his Bible and listening to God."

"Is he doing that now?"

"Well, no."

Actually, despite my adverse reaction to Nick's God thing, I couldn't deny that he had been a better husband the last number of weeks. Not that I gave him much credit for it, but he had been more attentive, a little less selfish, and certainly more emotionally present. *And he is taking some time off to take care of a two-year-old, which really is a miracle.*

"Learning to love well takes time," Jay said, "because it means laying down our selfish interests and living for the sake of another. That's a major shift. So you can't put a timetable on it. It's not like learning in a classroom."

"But..." *This is going to sound petty.* "It annoys me when Nick gets up at six o'clock now on Wednesdays. He has this men's group that he's started to go to. It's kind of a Bible study, I guess. I don't know. It's just so unlike Nick."

He laughed. "You don't expect Nick to teach himself, do you? Has it occurred to you that maybe these guys will actually help Nick learn to experience God deeply and so love you better?"

"That's the last thing that would have occurred to me."

"You know, you haven't realized it, but Nick's side of this marriage is taking care of itself. He will end up being a better husband than you ever thought he could be. The question now is, will you start growing into the kind of wife you could be? The only way you can do that is to have God himself living in you and to learn to hear his voice."

I hadn't been paying attention to our flight, and I was

startled when the plane landed with a jolt. We taxied briefly. I sat, thinking.

We stopped at the gate. As usual, everyone rose. A Hispanic couple with a child and an infant stood up across the aisle from us. The mother looked toward the bin above us.

Jay stood up and said something to her in fluent Spanish. She smiled, pointed at the bin, and said something in reply. Jay reached overhead and pulled out two small suitcases and set them in the aisle.

He turned back toward me.

I stood as well. "How many languages do you speak?"

"All of them."

"What do you mean, all of them?"

"I mean all of them."

"All the languages there are?"

"Yes."

"Say something in Mandarin for me."

He spoke in what sounded like Chinese. I wasn't sure what to say. "No one can know every language. There are thousands of them."

"I can."

I just stared at him.

"I've had a lot of time to practice, so to speak."

The aisle had cleared almost to our row. Jay leaned toward me. "We were talking about listening to God."

"Uh-huh."

"Would you like to practice a little?"

"Sure, I suppose." I had no idea where this was going.

He half whispered just above the noise of the passengers. "When your sister, Julie, has a baby boy one day, tell her not to worry about clothing. She can borrow yours."

"But I have a girl."

"I know. But starting in January, you'll have plenty of boy clothes. Congratulations, by the way." He smiled broadly, turned into the aisle, and walked off the plane.

I stood, motionless and speechless. *I haven't told anyone that—not even Nick.*

After a few seconds I snapped out of my daze. I gathered my things as quickly as I could. Three people went by in the aisle before I finally cut in front of someone, virtually knocking her out of the way. *Sorry. I have someone to catch.* I rushed down the aisle, pulling my suitcase behind me, then darted past a group of people in the jet bridge leading into the terminal.

"Sorry. Sorry!"

I burst into the terminal and looked to the right, then to

the left, then straight ahead. *No one.* I looked in every direction again. *Nothing.*

I glanced at the signs above me. Ground transportation was to the right. I ran past the gates and the shops and all the people waiting for their next destination. My eyes scanned to and fro while my brain processed clues from the last few hours.

And then it hit me—what had been right before my eyes the whole time.

I bolted toward the end of the terminal. Seeing an information counter, I veered over.

"Where are the hotel vans?" I asked, out of breath. *He'll be at the shuttle pickup,* I reassured myself.

The man pointed me to a waiting area outside. Pulling my suitcase, I ran out, dodged two cars dropping off people, and arrived at the shuttle lane. The bench there was empty. I looked to my left. A couple of lanes over and a little way down, I saw a familiar face. A taxi was slowing to pick him up.

I left my luggage behind as I sprinted toward the taxi. "Wait!" I cried out. "Wait!"

The man spoke to the taxi driver through the passenger-side window for a moment, then turned toward me as I approached the cab. But he was a stranger.

"Oh," I said, "I'm sorry. I thought you were a friend of mine."

"No problem." He opened the cab's door and slid inside.

I walked back toward my luggage. *Why couldn't that have been him? Did he just disappear?* I looked to my right, through the glass doors into the terminal. Nothing. The thought crossed my mind that maybe I should check baggage claim. *But he didn't have a thing with him. He probably didn't have any luggage at all. Why would he need luggage?*

I heard a vehicle approaching. I glanced back over my shoulder and saw my shuttle. I picked up my pace, but the shuttle got to the bench before I did.

"Hold on a sec!" I shouted as I got within range.

The shuttle driver appeared from behind the van and walked over to my luggage. I noticed his dreadlocks as he reached for the suitcase.

"Do you want the little bag with you or in the back?"

His accent sounded Jamaican. *Or at least what Jamaican is supposed to sound like.*

"I'll keep it, thanks."

He put my suitcase in the back of the van. I looked inside the front. It was empty. I sat in the row behind the driver's seat. The Jamaican took his seat and shifted into drive.

"Could you wait here for just a minute?" I asked. "Somebody else might join us."

"Sure thing," the driver answered. He glanced at me in the rearview mirror. I looked out the window, hoping to see Jay's face. *He even called himself Jay. How could I be so blind?*

The driver started humming a tune. A minute passed. He straightened slightly. "Ready to go, or should I wait a little longer?"

I took one last look around, then fighting off a pang of disappointment, said, "You can go."

The van pulled out and started toward the airport exit. The driver turned on some reggae music. I pondered.

Why did he leave like that? At least Nick got to figure out who he was and ask him some questions. Why did he wait until the end to make his identity obvious?

And why did he appear to me at all? Or to Nick? It's not like we're something special. Does he connect with people all the time?

As I thought it over, I felt astounded by the encounter and let down all at the same time. *Now what? What do you do after this kind of experience? Would anything else on earth come close?* My mind raced, running through the conversation we'd had.

We arrived at the resort. I checked in and made my way to my room—quite a hike, given the size of the place. I tried scoping out the place a little during my walk, but work was the last thing on my mind.

My room was spacious and elegant. *As I expected.* I parked my suitcase at the foot of the bed and freshened up a bit in the bathroom. I walked back into the bedroom and sat on the bed. I looked over at the phone and noticed a box covered with wrapping paper. I picked it up. On the top, tucked under the ribbon, was a small card with "Mattie" written on it. It wasn't Nick's handwriting.

I unwrapped the box first and looked inside. The present was wrapped in tissue paper. I pulled aside the paper and held up a darling blue newborn outfit. A white sheep decorated the front.

I reached for the envelope and pulled out the card. I opened it and read the words handwritten on the inside:

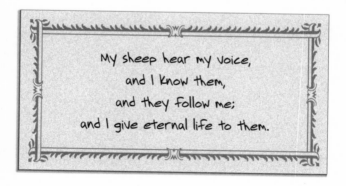

> My sheep hear my voice,
> and I know them,
> and they follow me;
> and I give eternal life to them.

About the Author

DAVID GREGORY is the author of *Dinner with a Perfect Stranger: An Invitation Worth Considering* and the coauthor of two nonfiction books. After a ten-year business career, he returned to school to study religion and communications, earning two master's degrees. David is a native of Texas.

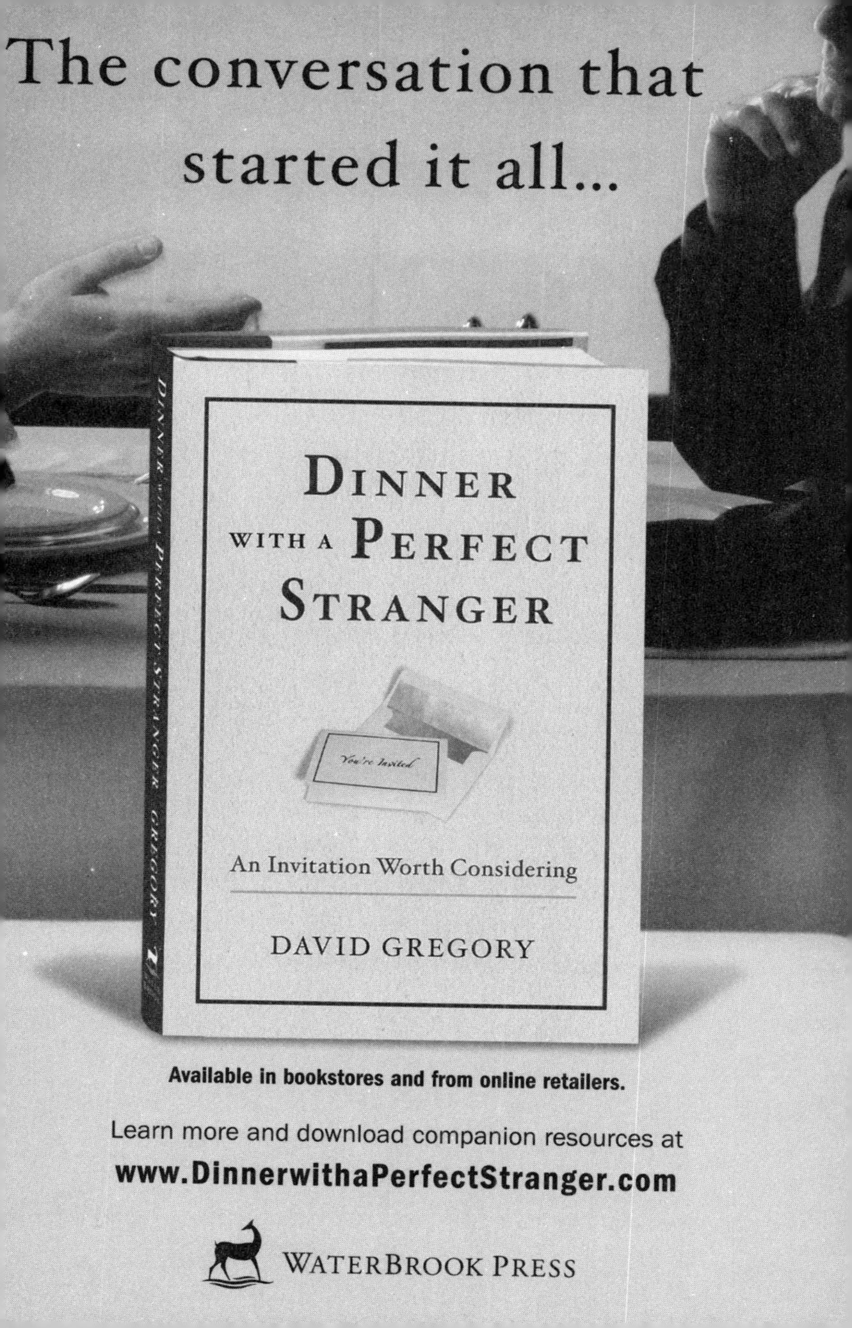
The conversation that
started it all...
DINNER
WITH A PERFECT
STRANGER
You're Invited
An Invitation Worth Considering
DAVID GREGORY
Available in bookstores and from online retailers.
Learn more and download companion resources at
www.DinnerwithaPerfectStranger.com
WATERBROOK PRESS

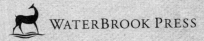

Praise for

Dinner with a Perfect Stranger

"Here's a wonderful feast for the mind and soul! Pull up a chair and eavesdrop on this provocative conversation. If you're like me, you'll hear questions that match your own—and answers that can change your life."

—LEE STROBEL, author of *The Case for Christ, The Case for Faith,* and *The Case for a Creator*

"There's just one thing people need in order to live a happy, abundant life: to be convinced that God loves them. Want to be convinced? Read *Dinner with a Perfect Stranger.* The author deftly anticipates and answers every question. I predict this little book will become a classic—one of a handful of modern books (like *Mere Christianity*) that people read to kindle or rekindle faith. All of the "business" surrounding the dinner is done so well it reminds me of *Babette's Feast*—simple, earthy details that profoundly convey spiritual reality. *Dinner with a Perfect Stranger* is truly a wonderful book that makes me feel I've just heard the gospel for the very first time."

—MIKE MASON, author of *The Mystery of Marriage, Champagne for the Soul,* and *Practicing the Presence of People*

"The choice is yours: Enjoy a delicious meal of, say, veal fantarella with grilled vegetables. Or spend a quiet hour reading David Gregory's book. You may find an altogether different sort of hunger has been sated by the final page. Brilliant in its simplicity, fearless in its presentation of the truth, *Dinner with a Perfect Stranger* is one invitation you'll want to RSVP."

—LIZ CURTIS HIGGS, author of *Thorn in My Heart, Fair Is the Rose,* and *Whence Came a Prince*

Dinner with a Perfect Stranger

Dinner with a Perfect Stranger

An Invitation Worth Considering

DAVID GREGORY

WaterBrook
Press

DINNER WITH A PERFECT STRANGER
PUBLISHED BY WATERBROOK PRESS
12265 Oracle Boulevard, Suite 200
Colorado Springs, Colorado 80921
A division of Random House, Inc.

10 Digit ISBN: 1-57856-905-2
13 Digit ISBN: 978-1-57856-905-2

Library of Congress Cataloging-in-Publication Data
Gregory, David, 1959-
Dinner with a perfect stranger : an invitation worth considering / David Gregory.—1st WaterBrook ed.
p. cm.
ISBN 1-57856-905-2
1. Jesus Christ—Fiction. 2. Dinners and dining—Fiction. 3. Restaurants—Fiction. 4. Imaginary conversations. I. Title.

PS3607.R4884D56 2005
813'.6—dc22

2005001761

Printed in the United States of America
2007

20 19 18 17 16 15 14

To Rick and Denise,
who made this book possible

Acknowledgments

My thanks to Howard Hendricks, Reg Grant, Scott Horrell, and Mike Moore for providing inspiration to venture outside my box, and to Sandi Glahn for coaching me.

To those who provided feedback on the manuscript, the readers say thanks (I hope). So do I. My special thanks to Rex Purkerson and Mallory Dubuclet for your unique contributions and to Bruce Nygren for seeing this project through to completion.

In the dog days of manuscript editing, every writer needs a downpour of encouragement to get through the final stages. Dad, you provided that encouragement.

Finally, to my wife, Ava, thank you for all your help with ideas and editing, for your patience, and for your contagious excitement about this book. You are a wonderful partner and a keen editor to boot.

1

The Invitation

I SHOULD HAVE known better than to respond. My personal planner was full enough without accepting anonymous invitations to dine with religious leaders. Especially dead ones.

Amid a stack of credit card applications and professional society junk, the invitation arrived at my work address:

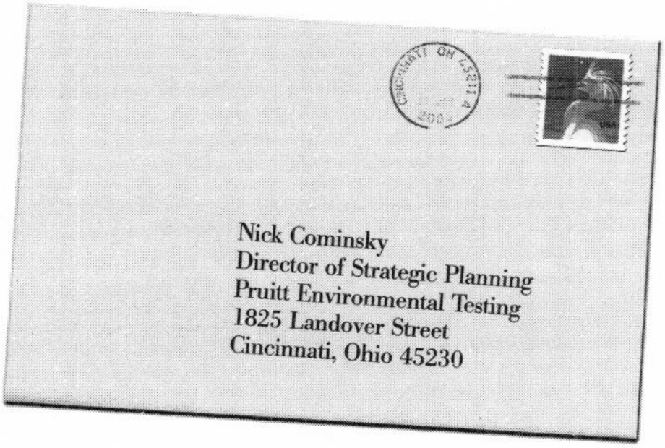

It came typeset on beige Crane paper with matching envelope. No return address. No RSVP.

You are invited

to a dinner

with

Jesus of Nazareth

Milano's Restaurant

Tuesday, March 24 • Eight o'clock

At first I thought the church down the street was having another one of their "outreaches." We had been outreached on more than one occasion. Their mailbox flier awaited us the minute my wife, Mattie, and I moved here from Chicago three years ago. An endless stream of what some church worker considered promotional material followed. I actually started looking forward to them, just for the amusement the sermon titles provided:

The Ten Commandments, Not the Ten Suggestions
If God Seems Far Away, Guess Who Moved?
Spiritual Aerobics for the Marathon to Heaven

Did they mean to attract anyone with those or just make the neighborhood disdain them?

Then came the events: the church bowling-league invitation, the spaghetti cookoff, the marriage-retreat weekend, the golf-scramble invitation. In a moment of insanity I actually broke down and went to the golf scramble. Utter agony is the only way to describe it. Parking at the course behind a guy with a "My Boss Is a Jewish Carpenter" bumper sticker set the tone. As it turned out, I was assigned to his foursome. He had this perpetual smile, as though someone had hit him with a brick and the plastic surgeon had patched him up on an off day. As for the other two, one guy shot a nice front nine but fell apart on the back nine and started swearing every time he hit a shot. I learned he headed the deacon board. The other guy never said a word except to track our score. He must have chaired the welcoming committee. That was the last church invitation I accepted.

So if that church had concocted it, there was no way I was going to this bogus dinner. But the more I thought about it, the more I concluded that someone else had sent the invitation. For one thing, how would the church have my work address? They were persistent but not particularly resourceful. For another, this just wasn't that church's style. The spaghetti cookoff was more their bag than Milano's, an upscale Italian restaurant. Besides, they would never send an anonymous invitation. If there was one thing they wanted you to know, it was that *their* church was sponsoring an event.

That left me in a quandary. Who would send me such an odd invitation? I called the restaurant, but they denied knowing anything. Of course, the staff could have agreed to play dumb about it, so that told me little. Cincinnati had lots of other churches, but I'd successfully avoided all contact with them. Our friends Dave and Paula went to the Unity Church, but they wouldn't invite me to something like this without Mattie.

One logical set of culprits remained: the guys at work. Les and Bill in particular were always putting together something crazy, like my bachelor party at a local mortuary and my guy baby shower (thankfully, they left Mattie off the invitation list; I'd never seen such a raunchy celebration for the birth of a baby). I admit, this invitation seemed a bit strange even for those guys. And they should have known better than to send me the invitation at work. It was too obvious. Otherwise they had done a pretty good job: classy envelope and printing, bizarre event, nice restaurant.

I decided to play it cool with them, never mentioning the invite. And for three full weeks they kept cool too, letting slip not so much as a sly grin. As the twenty-fourth approached, my anticipation grew, wondering what their fertile imaginations had conceived this time.

Only one thing stood between the dinner and me: Mattie. Three seventy-hour workweeks had already placed me deep in the doghouse with my other half, who chafed at even my usual sixty-hour pace. I couldn't think how to justify a night out with the guys, leaving her home again with Sara, our daughter.

Granted, it's hard looking after a twenty-month-old by yourself all day and then all evening, too. Not to mention that Mattie ran a home graphics business on the side. If we had stayed in Chicago, either of our mothers could have helped her out with Sara. Well, hers anyway. My mother would have squealed at the chance to keep the baby, but staying at her house too often would probably have made Sara...like me. Hopefully, the three hundred miles between Cincinnati and Chicago sufficiently insulated my daughter from that fate.

Mattie knew when she moved to Cincinnati with me and we married that I'd be working long hours. You can't have a job like mine and clock out at five. I can just imagine waving my hand at Jim, my boss, as I pass by his office on my way out. "Sorry, man, got to go again. Mattie needs me home at five thirty to dice Sara's vegetables." A few five o'clock departures and Jim would insist I stay home as a full-time nanny.

I can see my résumé now:

Education

BS, Chemistry, Northern Illinois University, 1996

MBA, Northwestern University, 2001

Work History

Research Chemist, Abbott Laboratories, 1996–2000

Corporate Planning Analyst, Abbott Laboratories, 2000–2002

Director of Strategic Planning, Pruitt Environmental Testing, 2002–2005

Nanny, 2005 to present

Keeping my current job seemed preferable, despite the dangers it presented. Truth was, between the pile on my desk at work and Mattie's perpetual displeasure at home, getting away from both for an evening appealed to me. I just wondered whether Milano's knew what it was getting into with Les's and Bill's antics.

The restaurant's problems were far from my mind, though, as I approached its parking lot. Mattie shouting into the cell phone, "Nick, I might as well be a single parent for all you—" were the last words I heard on the way over before static saved me. That was enough. I never had figured out how to rationalize my plans for the evening. In retrospect, I should have given her more than twenty minutes' notice.

Blasting some R.E.M. while speeding down Anderson Ferry didn't completely drown my guilt, but it gave it a good dunking. I pulled the Explorer into the parking lot, cut the engine, and reached once more for the invitation, hoping it would give me one last hint about what to expect for the evening. It didn't. Suddenly nothing about this dinner seemed worth the cold shoulder I would get from Mattie later on.

I was here, though. And if the whole event was a wash-out, I could save face with Mattie by leaving early. Showing up at home sooner than expected at least once a month seemed to buy me a little grace. After the last three weeks, I needed some—badly.

Contingency plan in hand, I crossed the parking lot, breached the threshold, and glanced around the twenty or so tables. No guys with long hair in flowing robes. No guys from work, either.

2

The Seating

"DINNER FOR ONE, sir?"

The maître d's appearance from behind the wine bar dashed my option of bolting before anyone noticed me.

"Sir? Dinner for one?"

"No, I'm...I'm supposed to meet someone. I'm Nick Cominsky..."

"Ah, Mr. Cominsky. Right this way."

He grabbed a menu and led me past the wood lattice that bordered the single dining room. The place hadn't changed since I had brought Mattie for Valentine's two years back. Two staggered tablecloths, one white and one red, covered each of the tables. Large mirrors created the image of a side dining area. The windows on two sides of the room overlooked the Ohio River. I could see lights from the Kentucky side reflecting on the water. The current provided nice background noise, like those ocean CDs you can buy to help you sleep. Unfortunately, some lame Andrea Bocelli song that Mattie loved virtually drowned out the river.

Tuesdays looked slow at Milano's. Guests occupied only four tables. I inhaled the smell of toasted bread as we passed an older party of six laughing at a front table. A couple in their early twenties held hands and made goo-goo eyes at each other in the far right corner, the guy oblivious to his shirt sleeve dangling in his ravioli. In the middle of the room, two weight-challenged women giggled as they plunged into a monstrous chocolate torte. And in the far corner on the left, a thirty-something man in a blue business suit sat by himself, perusing a menu.

The maître d' led me over to him. Rising from his chair, he stuck out his hand and firmly grasped mine.

"Nick Cominsky," he said. "Hi. Jesus."

In retrospect, a thousand comebacks were possible—"Jesus H. Christ! So good to finally meet you!"..."Are twelve of our party missing?"..."I didn't know they buried you in a suit."

The absurdity of the scene, though, stunned me into silence. What do you say to that? The man and I continued shaking hands a little too long, until I issued a weak "Uh-huh." He released my hand and sat back down.

My eyes caught the maître d's. He quickly averted his

glance and picked my napkin off my plate, cueing me to sit. He placed the napkin in my lap, handed me a menu and, with an "Enjoy your dinner," left me alone with...

"Thanks for meeting me," the man started. "This probably wasn't the most convenient time for you, middle of the week."

We stared at each other. Well, I stared. He resumed looking at his menu. He had an average build and was a little shorter than me, maybe five foot ten or so. His complexion toned olive, his hair dark and wavy, cut short and combed forward. His bushy eyebrows (*Mattie would make me trim those,* I thought) hung over deep eye sockets and brown eyes dark enough that you couldn't quite tell where the iris ended and the pupil began. His slender nose and thinnish lips matched a chin that receded slightly, as if knowing it couldn't compete with the brows above. He wasn't *GQ* cover material, but he definitely spent more time in the gym than I did. His suit wasn't Armani, but it wasn't Discount Warehouse, either.

He looked up and caught me scrutinizing him, but he didn't seem the least bit uncomfortable. Since my eyes provided few clues as to what this whole thing was about, I decided to give my ears a shot.

"Excuse me, but am I supposed to know you?"

"That's a good question," he smiled, to himself I guess. "I would say the answer is yes."

"I'm sorry, but I've never met you, as far as I can remember."

"That's true."

I looked around the room, waiting for the guys to jump out from behind the lattice or maybe from the men's room. But no one hid behind the lattice. As for the men's room... I turned my attention to the guy across the table.

"Come at me again. You are..."

"Jesus. My family called me Yeshua."

"Your family, from..."

"Nazareth."

"Of course."

"Well, I grew up there. I wasn't born there."

"No, of course not. That would have been in..."

"Bethlehem. But we didn't stay long before we left for Egypt."

That was about all I needed to hear. This guy was a nut. Without saying a word, I got up, retraced my steps past the lattice, took a right, and entered the bathroom. Mr. Ravioli was rinsing off his sleeve, but besides him, no one. Backing out, I momentarily considered cracking the door to the women's room, but I wasn't that desperate to find Les and Bill. I took a left and peeked through the circular window to the kitchen. Nothing. I paused, scanned the restaurant, and, deciding this warranted a more direct approach, returned to the table.

"Look," I said, sitting on the edge of my chair, "I've got better things to do tonight than have some mystery dinner with… Who are you really, and what's going on here?" My question had an unintended edge. After all, the guy hadn't done anything to me except meet for dinner.

"I know this isn't quite what you expected. But I think if you give this evening a try, you'll find it meaningful."

"Of course!" I retorted. "Who wouldn't find a dinner with Jesus meaningful? Last week I had dinner with Napoleon. Socrates the week before. But Jesus! Thank you so much for coming all the way from the Holy Land!" I realized my voice was carrying more than I wanted. The two women had turned our way.

He sat silently.

"Hey"—I rose again from my chair—"I need to get home to my wife and daughter. Thanks for the invitation." I stuck out my hand in a conciliatory gesture.

"Mattie went out to a movie with Jill," he said without flinching. "She got Rebecca to baby-sit Sara."

Okay. Finally a few pieces were starting to fall into place. He knew my wife. He knew Jill Conklin, the wife of my best friend, Chris. He knew our regular baby-sitter, Rebecca. He knew Mattie and Jill had gone to a movie. Once more I reclaimed my seat.

"Did Chris put you up to this?" I couldn't imagine how Chris could be involved; it was way too weird for him.

"No, he didn't."

I returned to my original suspects. "Are you a friend of Bill Grier and Les Kassler?"

He slid his menu aside and leaned forward. "I'll tell you what. If you stay for dinner, I promise to tell you at the end who set it up."

The last time Bill and Les had done something like this, I ended up wearing fake cement overshoes and getting tossed into a swimming pool on Halloween. A heated pool, fortunately. Now I was having dinner with some guy claiming to be Jesus.

The waiter interrupted my thoughts, addressing the man across the table. "Have you selected a wine, sir?"

"I think I'll let my friend decide," he responded, turning to me. "Would you care for some wine?"

"Who's paying?"

"I am."

"Okay," I replied, "sure."

I opened the wine list and scanned thirty or so offerings, none of which I recognized. I was tempted to order the most expensive one on the list, but instead I pointed to a midrange white. "We'll take the Kalike."

I handed the wine list to the waiter. He looked back at my host, who gave a slight nod.

"The Vermentino di Gallura–Kalike '98," the waiter confirmed to me. He departed, passing a busboy with a water pitcher. The busboy filled my glass first, then the other guy's, eliciting a "Thank you, Carlo."

We both picked up our water glasses and took a drink. I had to admit, this guy was good. Where did they find someone willing to play Jesus for an evening? And in such an unassuming way, as if he were just a normal guy. My coworkers had outdone themselves this time. But why? What was the point to all this? Les and Bill weren't particularly religious. Bill went to Mass on Christmas and Easter, when his wife dragged him there. As for Les, he worshiped only at Western Hills Country Club.

Glancing back over at the pre-honeymooners, the mirror caught my eye. Could the restaurant have a two-way mirror? That seemed a little far-fetched, but no more so than the evening had been thus far.

Our waiter appeared behind me with a bottle of wine, opened it, and set the cork down for me. I picked it up and took a whiff. "Smells good." I looked up at him, detecting a slight roll of his eyes.

He poured a small amount into my wineglass and handed it to me to taste. Mattie and I frequently had wine at home but not in this class. "Very nice."

He poured me a full glass, then one across the table before leaving the bottle, prompting a "Thank you, Eduardo" this time. *Is he on a first-name basis with the entire wait staff? He must come here weekly.*

I was tempted to ask, but I had already decided on a different strategy. I leaned back in my chair and turned to "Jesus," suppressing my customary sarcastic smile. "So your family called you Yeshua?"

"Most of them. James called me a few other things."

"Well, Yesh— Do you mind if I call you Yesh?"

"Whatever suits you."

"Yesh it is, then. Tell me,"—I held up my wineglass—"can you turn this wine back into water?"

3

The Menu

"NO PROBLEM," HE replied. He turned and signaled for the waiter, who came to the table. "My friend would like a second glass of water instead of this wine."

With a "Certainly, sir," the waiter removed my wineglass and turned to retrieve water.

"Very funny," I muttered before calling after the waiter. "I think I'll keep my wine."

"Very well, sir." He returned the glass to the table.

"Thank you, Eduardo," my host said. "Sorry to bother you."

Eduardo departed. I opened my menu and momentarily buried myself in it. The quality of the dinner conversation was doubtful, but not the caliber of the food. Guests selected a four-course meal: an appetizer, a salad, an entrée, and later a dessert. I gave half of my attention to my order, the other half to contemplating what I was still doing here. My growling stomach answered that question; I had worked straight through lunch.

"What do you think?"

I lowered my menu enough to peek over it. "I think I'm crazy for not leaving when I had the chance."

"About your order."

Last time we came Mattie ordered something really good. What was it?

"The veal," I finally responded. I plopped the menu down, emphasizing my one accomplishment so far that night—deciding what to eat.

"I'll go with the salmon."

"Is this a Friday?"

A slight smile curled his lips. "Touché," he said.

He placed his menu on the table, and the waiter appeared immediately.

"Are you ready to order, sir?" he asked me.

"Yes. I'll take the stuffed mushrooms, the Mediterranean salad, and veal fantarella."

"Certainly." He turned to my dinner partner. "And you, sir?"

"I would like the tomato and artichoke soup, the tortellini salad, and the salmon filet, please."

An upgrade from his usual bread and wine, to say the least.

As the waiter walked off with our menus, "Jesus" leaned

back in his chair, took a sip of wine, and made a first stab at initiating real conversation. "Tell me about your family."

"I thought you knew everything already." I dodged the question. "You had Judas figured out. Didn't help you much, if I may say so."

He probably assumed I didn't know anything about religion or the Bible, but I'd served my time in Sunday school. I'd hated every minute of it, of course. After Mother drove Dad away, she used to take Ellen, Chelle, and me to church. She'd tell us, "We need a good influence, for once." Stacy, sixteen by then, refused to go. I should have too, but being younger, I wielded limited power.

So I went. The lessons served as background noise to the real activities of passing notes, throwing spit wads at the girls, and stealing from the "junior" collection plate. The teachers were mostly nondescript—a few men who wore pasted-on smiles, trying to make it seem as though they actually wanted to be there, and women who thought that boys actually enjoyed flannelboard Bible stories.

One lady, Mrs. Willard, was a classic. Her mantra was "love one another as yourself." Yet the minute someone so much as twitched an eyebrow, she'd grab him by the ear, drag him to the front, and make him write a hundred "I will do unto others as I would have them do unto me." Maybe that's what she did want others to do unto her.

I learned little by example at church, but a few Bible stories did seep through: the Good Samaritan, the Bad Samaritan, the Mediocre Samaritan. I'd caught enough to keep up with this guy for a while.

"Why don't you humor me?" he answered, ignoring my Judas reference. "Where is your family from?"

I wasn't about to let him off the hook that easily. After all, he was the one claiming to be Jesus. Now he had to play the part.

"I'm much more interested in your family, Yesh." I felt a smirk creep onto my face. "Tell me about Joseph and Mary."

He jumped right in. "Growing up in Nazareth wasn't exactly like boyhood in Chicago. We didn't go for foot-long hot dogs and Cracker Jacks at Wrigley."

"Oh, really?" I responded sarcastically. What I didn't say was, *Funny he picked Chicago, and Wrigley Field, where Dad and I went every Saturday.*

He continued. "Joseph was a good father. He had to work a lot, but it wasn't like today. His shop next to the house had an unhurried pace. Joseph only sped up when he heard me coming. He always tried to finish a project before I could get my hands on it."

He put his hand on his chin, looked away, and laughed. "I didn't realize at the time how many of his pieces I used to mess up. He'd be making a table or something, and I'd want to help. Needless to say, at eight I wasn't exactly a master carpenter. He'd go back and redo some from scratch that I had 'helped' on. Other pieces he'd go ahead and use. Some of the neighbors kindly accepted items that had my unique imprint."

Half of me listened to this spiel; the other half analyzed him. The guys must have hired a professional actor for this part. He actually talked like he had grown up in Nazareth. This guy was *good.*

I was going to ask about Mary when the waiter appeared with a loaf of hot bread and some spinach spread. "Jesus" reached for the bread knife, cut a slice, and held the board toward me.

"Some bread?"

I took the slice and tried some of the spread before proceeding with the family history. "So Joseph was just a regular Joe. And Mary—it must have been rough growing up with such a revered mom."

He chuckled, either slightly amused or annoyed—I couldn't tell which. "She was hardly revered. More like an outcast when I was young. Having a child before the wedding was not—"

"Kosher," I interjected, trying to get in the Jewish spirit of things.

He paused. "It wasn't the thing to do."

"From all the paintings it seems like Mary was always either seeing angels or nursing you or taking you off the cross. Did she do anything in between?"

The question was a bit over the top, I guess. But I had to do something to rock this guy out of his routine. He acted way too natural. Even this didn't faze him, though. He just took some more bread and went on talking.

"I had a great mother. Her faith kept her going—and her sense of humor. She never let me live down my remark as a kid that I had to be about my Father's business. Someone would come to our house looking for me. 'I don't know where he is,' she would say. 'About his Father's business.' The older I got, the more she would say, 'Do you think your Father's business might involve finding a girl and settling down?' "

A smile crossed his face as he talked. He paused, then got more serious. "When I finally started preaching, it got hard for her, seeing her son worshiped one day and demonized the next. It was harder for her than she expected."

Maybe she should have gone on Dr. Phil's show. He probably could have helped her out. I was finding this routine a little wearing.

"Look, you haven't told me anything that someone with

a Bible and half an imagination couldn't make up. You're going to have to come up with something better than these sappy Joseph and Mary stories."

"To do what?" he asked.

That was a good question. What exactly did I expect from a guy pretending to be Jesus? I guess something a little more interesting. Larry King once said that of all the personalities in history, he would most like to have interviewed Jesus. Talking with Jesus Christ—or even his impostor—should have been more engaging than this. Surely this guy had something in mind other than rehashing old Bible stories.

His voice snapped me back to the conversation. "I don't think there's much I can say that would actually convince you I'm Jesus."

"Well, that's one true statement."

"I have a suggestion. Why don't you suspend your disbelief for a while and proceed as if I am Jesus? Surely if Jesus were actually here, you might have some questions for him."

That wasn't a bad idea. We were getting nowhere with my trying to figure out his real identity. And this had the potential to be interesting. Assuming this guy knew his stuff, this might be the best philosophical discussion I'd had since...Northern Illinois days? We actually used to talk about Kant and Kierkegaard and even Feynman back then.

The closest thing I got to that now were those ridiculous parenting books that Mattie force-fed me.

"Okay, fine," I replied. "I have one for you. The other day I passed by the church down the street, and their sign read, '"No one comes to the Father but through me"—Jesus.' If you actually said that, I think you're full of it."

4

The Appetizer

"YOUR TOMATO AND artichoke soup, sir."

I cringed. The waiter's intrusion had ruined the whole setup. I had just landed my first blow, had this fraud reeling, when the interruption gave him time to regroup. His dish was served first. Then Eduardo brought mine around and set a plate in front of me.

"Your stuffed mushrooms."

I looked across the table where "Jesus" sat, making no move toward his utensils. *Oh, great. Now what's he going to do—ask me to say grace?*

"I usually say a short word of thanks before meals. Do you mind?"

"Whatever" was my preferred response, but "No, not at all" was what came out.

He raised his head toward the ceiling and left his eyes

open. I couldn't help but follow his gaze, wondering if I had missed something up there. I hadn't.

"Father, thank you for always providing for us, whom you love." He lowered his head, took a spoon in his hand, and dipped into his soup.

"That's it?" I asked.

"Is there something else you would like to say?"

"No. No, I guess that covers it." I grabbed a fork and speared one of the mushrooms.

We sat silently for a number of moments, eating our appetizers. I debated how to circle back to my question when my host solved the problem for me.

"Why do you think I'm mistaken?" he asked.

"Because here you've got all these people around the world who believe in all these different things and worship God in all these different ways, and Jesus claimed only his way was the right one?"

"And your difficulty with that is..."

"A lot. Who is to say that Jesus's way was any better than Muhammad's or Buddha's or Confucius's or... Well, there really wasn't a specific Hindu guy." *Did he pick up on the fact that I knew which religions had a founder and which did not?*

"Do you think Hinduism is true?" he inquired.

"I don't know. My friends Dave and Paula have gotten into some Hindu stuff, and it seems to work for them."

He reached for another piece of bread and applied some spinach spread. "I didn't ask if you thought it worked. I asked if you thought it was true."

"Well, it's true for them."

He took a bite of his bread and seemed to ponder how to respond. "Before Copernicus, most people believed the earth was flat. That was false, but it worked for them. Why?"

"I suppose it didn't matter much back then. Until Columbus, they never traveled far enough for it to be a problem. Well, except for the Vikings."

"And what if humanity had tried to go to the moon while still believing the earth was flat?"

"So you're saying…"

"What people believed worked for them, to a point, even though it wasn't true. But at some critical juncture it ceased to work anymore."

"And…"

"You tell me. You're the one with the master's degree."

"In business, not philosophy."

"You had to think a little." He reached for his spoon.

I wasn't sure how I'd gotten off the offensive and was now playing near my own goal line, but I decided I might as well go along. Besides, I admit I was starting to find the conversation a tad intriguing. "What you're saying is that even if a belief system seems to work for someone, if it's false, eventually it will break down."

He leaned forward. "And you don't want what you're ultimately trusting to be wrong." He paused a moment, then leapfrogged forward. "Now, you're the scientist."

"Used to be."

"And you took that comparative religion class at Northern Illinois. What do you think? How does Hinduism line up with what you know about the universe?"

"How did you—," I started to respond. *But what's the point? He seems to have this whole scene, including me, thoroughly researched. I just hope there's a limit to what he's found out.* I returned to the question. "As I recall, Hinduism teaches that the universe is simply an extension of this universal force called..."

"Brahman."

"Yeah, Brahman, the ultimate essence."

"So God is the universe, and the universe is God."

"Right. There is no separate creator."

He slid back in his chair. "And how long has the universe existed?"

"Well, some Hindus would say always. Brahman is eternal, so the universe is eternal."

"How does that match what your astronomers have discovered in the last century?"

I pondered that one for a moment. "Not too well," I admitted. Although I had loved cosmology in college (I would have majored in astronomy if I could have made any money at it), I hadn't thought down this path before. "All the evidence points to the fact that the universe had an actual beginning in time, maybe fifteen billion years ago."

"What if that number is wrong?"

"The universe still can't be eternal. The second law of thermodynamics. In a closed system, everything eventually winds down. In an infinitely old universe, we wouldn't see new stars or galaxies forming. It all would have wound down, with no productive energy remaining. A couple of people, like Hoyle, tried to hold on to the steady-state theory, in which the universe would be eternal, but no one accepts it anymore."

"Jesus" leaned forward and entwined his fingers on the table. "So if Hinduism is true, how did the universe get here?"

"I don't know."

He smiled. "I don't know, either."

We took a couple of bites before he spoke again. "Hinduism's depiction of reality has other problems."

"Like what?"

"Morality, for one. Humans are highly moral beings. All societies, even primitive ones, have complex—and similar—moral codes."

"Agreed."

"Now, let me ask you this: what is the ultimate source of morality in Hinduism? Does Brahman establish right and wrong?"

I picked a piece of bread off my plate and thought about that one a second. "No, Brahman is amoral. With the universal force, nothing is ultimately right or wrong. It simply is."

"So what is the basis of morality if the source of all things is nonmoral? What makes anything inherently right or wrong?"

"We do, I suppose."

"But you are an extension of Brahman, which is amoral."

I didn't have a reply to that one. He continued. "Hinduism has a similar issue with personality. One of the things people appreciate most about themselves is their individuality. It's part of what it means to be human. Do you remember what Hinduism teaches about that?"

"Yeah. Personality is an illusion. You have to renounce it to enter into oneness with the universe."

"So what you most value about yourself is illusory. One

day you'll be reabsorbed into Brahman and lose your individuality."

I had to admit, that never had sounded all that appealing.

"If personality is an illusion," he asked, "why are people all so individual? How did an impersonal universal force bring forth such unique personalities?"

"But you could make these arguments about all Eastern religions."

"Yes. That's the problem with them. The world is not as they describe. They provide a way of understanding life, but it's a false understanding." He leaned back, wiping his mouth. "What do you remember about Buddhism?"

Buddhism was always a little easier to get a handle on than Hinduism. It was hard to forget the Four Noble Truths and the Eightfold Path. I couldn't name them all, but I did remember the main idea.

"Buddhism is kind of like Hinduism in its basic worldview," I said. "Ultimate reality is this...abstract void called nirvana. You enter nirvana by traveling an Eightfold Path and stamping out all attachment or desire in yourself. Once you've eliminated that, all your suffering ends."

He picked up his wineglass and held it in front of him, looking at the wine and then peering at me through the glass with a strangely distorted face. He moved the glass to the side of his vision. "Someone made this glass well. They were attached to a sense of fine craftsmanship."

"Probably."

"How much have humans accomplished without someone having passion?"

"Not much," I conceded.

"You've taken plenty of biology. How many sensory nerve cells do we have in our skin, capable of providing pleasure?"

"Millions."

"So somehow an impersonal universe has taken the form of personal beings with strong desires and the ability to feel great pleasure, and yet the goal of life is to negate all desire." He put the glass down.

"I suppose it doesn't make much sense," I said, making his point for him.

"Do you think that perhaps suffering was so great in India that Siddhartha Gautama, the Buddha, tried to come up with some explanation for it and developed an entire belief system based on alleviating suffering?"

My answer, or lack thereof, was preempted by the waiter appearing on my right. "Are you finished with your mushrooms, sir?"

I momentarily considered the two that remained. "Sure."

He removed our dishes, a well-timed interruption. Too much more talk about Eastern religions and my ignorance would start showing. One thing was certain. I wasn't going to play this guy in Trivial Pursuit, Religion Edition. At the risk of getting in over my head, I wanted to see what he would say about something closer to Christianity.

"What about Islam?" I asked. "Maybe pantheistic religions don't hold up. But Muslims claim to worship the God of the Bible. Who says that their version is wrong and Jesus was right?"

He reached for his water, then answered. "That depends on whether God actually spoke to Muhammad, doesn't it? That's a lot of weight to give one guy's writings, especially one who, after supposedly hearing from an angel, wasn't sure whether he had heard from God, had persistent bouts of suicidal thoughts, built a following based partly on military conquest, countenanced the murder of his enemies, and married a nine-year-old, among other things."

"Who says that? I've never heard those things, except the military part."

"Revered Muslim writings. The *Sirat Rasul Allah.* The Hadith collections of Bukhari, Muslim, and Abu Dawud. *The History of al-Tabari,* among others."

I didn't have any basis on which to argue the point with

him, so I returned to his original statement. "But you could say the same about Christianity, that it revolves around whether God spoke to some guy."

"No, the Bible has over forty authors spanning fifteen hundred years, all with a consistent message. That argues for, not against, a divine origin."

"Still, who's to say that God didn't speak to Muhammad?"

"If God did, he got some things wrong."

"Like what?"

"Muhammad wrote that I was never crucified, that God's angels rescued me and took me straight to heaven."

"You mean Jesus."

"That's what I said."

I decided not to rehash that debate. "So maybe Muhammad was right."

That elicited a slight smile. "No, he wasn't."

"Oh, of course. I forgot. You were there."

"But you don't have to ask me," he continued, ignoring my comment. "My crucifixion is historically documented, not only by early Christians, but also by non-Christian historians of the time. Throw it out, and you have to throw out everything you know about ancient history."

I couldn't disagree, actually. You could debate about the resurrection, but Jesus's crucifixion was a certainty. I was about to ask another question when he resumed.

"Islam teaches other things that aren't true."

"Such as?"

"That the Bible has been altered over time so that what you have now is a highly corrupted version that can't be trusted."

"So?"

"So that's false. Any scholar in the field will tell you that. The Dead Sea Scrolls, among other things, prove the reliability of the Hebrew Bible. And you have over five thousand early manuscripts that validate the New Testament. You have what the authors wrote. It's up to you what to do with it, but you have what they wrote."

He moved his wineglass toward the top of his place setting. "But that's not the biggest problem with Islam."

"Which is…"

He looked around the room for a second, scanning for I'm not sure what. His eyes returned to me. "What is your deepest desire?"

Where did that question come from? "I'm not sure I want to get into that."

"Then let's talk in generalities. What do people in their hearts most deeply long for?"

"A raise?" I kidded. All right, half kidded. He didn't respond.

I thought for a minute, glancing around the room

myself. The ravioli guy and his girl were still making cow eyes at each other across their cleared table. "I suppose people's greatest desire is to be loved." I looked back at my host.

He leaned forward, and his voice softened. "I don't mean to be too personal, Nick. But in your experience, has another person ever fulfilled your need for love?"

He is getting too personal, whether he wants to or not. Besides, I thought we were talking about Islam. I resisted the urge to look away again, though I did shift back in my chair. I thought of my dad, of Mattie, of Elizabeth, my girlfriend at NIU. "No, not really."

"That's because another person can never satisfy it. Only God can. He designed people that way. But Muslims never have that hope. You can't have a personal relationship with Allah. He is someone to worship and serve from afar, even in paradise. It doesn't meet the deepest need of humanity's heart. Why would God create humanity with this deep need, then never meet it?"

I kept my eyes on him for a moment, then picked up my wineglass and took a drink. "Maybe Muslims don't have all the answers. But I don't think anybody does."

"No, they don't. They only think they do."

He spoke not sarcastically or arrogantly but with almost a hint of sadness. Uncomfortable with the subsequent silence, I glanced toward the river but saw in the window only the reflection of my face and the back of his head.

"What if God doesn't even exist?" I looked back toward him. "Maybe the material world is all there is."

"Then you have the problem of design."

"What, that there's no way it could have happened by accident?" It was a common argument and, frankly, a good one.

"You're aware of Roger Penrose," he said.

"Yeah. Helped develop black hole theory."

"Do you know the odds he calculated of a cosmic accident producing this orderly universe rather than chaos?"

I hadn't read Penrose's calculation, but I had seen similar comments by Hawking, Dyson, and others. I guessed: "One in a million?"

"Try one in a hundred billion, to the one hundred twenty-third power."

"Not very good odds."

"And that's just the macrouniverse. He omits the design complexity of biological life."

He had me there. The more I'd studied cosmology, the more apparent the design in the universe had become. I thought those who promoted the idea of random chance had more of a philosophical ax to grind than science on their side.

I reached for a piece of bread, spread butter on it this

time, and took a bite. "Okay, fine. I agree that there has to be some transcendent being, not just physical existence. And you're great at poking holes in all these other religions. But it seems to me that all religions, including Christianity, are different paths to the same place. I mean, everyone is looking for God, and—"

"Are you?"

That interjection caught me by surprise. *Am I looking for God? You wouldn't think so, observing my life.* I decided to ignore his question.

"As I was saying, it seems like everyone is looking for God in their own way. That's what I like about the church our friends Dave and Paula attend. They embrace everyone's beliefs and try to help them on their path to God."

"There's one problem with that thinking," he said.

"What?"

"There is no path to God."

That was the last thing I expected to hear.

5

The Salad

TO MY RIGHT, the waiter lingered with our salads, for how long I don't know. Our pause cued his approach. Maybe he avoided interrupting "serious" conversations. I guess this one qualified. I wasn't quite sure how I got suckered into a God discussion, but it was more captivating than my college prof pontificating on comparative religion. Mr. Drone, we called him, for his preferred lecture style.

The tortellini salad across the table jogged my memory. *That was what Mattie had ordered that was so good. Oh, well.* I pulled my selection closer and reached for a new fork.

"Care for some tortellini?" my host asked, pointing to his own salad. Before I had a chance to respond, he reached over, grabbed my empty bread plate, scooped half of his portion onto it, and handed it to me.

"That's too much," I said in polite protest.

"This place serves enough food for two dinners. I have plenty."

He was right about the servings, and I wasn't about to argue. I took the dish and pushed my own salad to the side. "Thank you."

I took a bite. "This is ungodly."

He tasted it as well but didn't respond. I had a couple more bites before getting the conversation back on track.

"What do you mean, there's no path to God? Every religion claims to teach the way to God."

"Oh, there's a way to God," he said. "Just not a path."

He had lost me. From the look on my face, he probably knew it.

"What I mean is this: a path is something you travel down by your own effort to reach a destination. But there's no such path to God. There is nothing you can do to work your way to God. That path doesn't exist. It—"

"Wait a minute. That's what all religion is about, trying to get to God. How can you say otherwise?"

He took another couple of bites before responding. "Did you ever get into trouble as a kid?"

"Are we changing the subject?"

"We'll get back to the other."

I wasn't too sure I wanted to talk about me anymore, although in truth it was a favorite subject of mine. "I don't think this place stays open late enough for all my trouble-making history."

He smiled. "That bad? Give me a highlight."

I reached over to sample my own salad. My mind raced from getting my first spanking to playing Halloween pranks to teasing my sister Ellen to aborting a plan to smoke bomb the high-school teachers' lounge to… *No point in bringing up the present.* I backtracked.

"When I was four, my mother made these Christmas decorations—miniature drummer-boy drums. I don't know what she used them for. Anyway, she'd covered the sides with green and red crepe paper, plus somehow she had attached spearmint Life Savers on the sides."

He started smiling, probably knowing where this was heading.

"So she had them in the utility room, on the washer and dryer. And I snuck in there and plucked a Life Saver off one of the drums. Then I crossed through the kitchen, where Mother was, to get out. But a few minutes later I went back in, saying, 'I forgot something' as I entered the utility room. When I tried it a third time, my 'I forgot something again' wasn't too convincing."

I started chuckling to myself. "She opened the door, and there I was, stuffing my pockets with as many Life Savers as I could. That was the first spanking I remember. Actually, my dad did it when he got home. He always used to do it. He wasn't too mad, really. But Mother was, so he had to."

I paused, lost momentarily in my childhood. "Once Dad got really mad, though."

"When..."

"When I was about nine. My sister Chelle must've been five. We had stopped at a burger place for some ice cream, and Chelle wanted a big vanilla shake. Dad tried to talk her into a small one, but she insisted on a large. So we all got our orders, got back in the car, and drove off. Then Chelle started on her shake. But the thing was so thick that she couldn't use a straw. So she took the plastic top off and tilted it toward her mouth. Except it was barely moving, and she kept tilting it up farther and farther, and the main blob still wasn't moving. So finally I said, 'Come on, Chelle!' and reached over and gave the bottom of the cup a *whap.* When I did that, the whole thing came cascading onto her face. When she opened her eyes, all you could see were these two big, brown circles poking out through the white ice cream."

He started laughing with me. I continued. "She looked like a ghost. I burst out laughing, she burst out crying, and my dad burst out yelling—at me. He never used to do that, but this time he did. He slammed on the brakes, got out, wiped her off as best he could, then bent me over his knee and gave me my worst spanking ever. He was not happy."

I wiped my eyes with my napkin. I hadn't thought about that in years or laughed so hard in a while, either. "I think that was the last vanilla shake I ever saw Chelle get. She always ordered chocolate after that."

We both took a drink of water, looked at each other, and chuckled a bit more as we returned to our salads. Finally he got us back to semiserious conversation. "So your dad always handled the spanking."

"Yeah. Mother just screamed at us. But Dad didn't spank much. I probably didn't get half a dozen spankings growing up."

"Why not?"

"I don't know." I thought about that for a second. "I don't know. That just wasn't his way of handling things. Usually he made sure we understood why what we had done was wrong. Then he always made us apologize to the other person. Especially to Mother."

I took another bite of tortellini. He had a sip of wine, then said, "It sounds as though your dad had a lot in common with God."

That one cut short my next bite en route to my mouth. "How so?"

"They both focused on restoring relationships."

I wasn't quite getting the connection. "Meaning…"

"Your dad had you admit how you had hurt someone

and apologize. He was interested in restoring relationships."

I guess that's true. I've never thought about it that way.

"God is like that," he continued. "He's not interested in people trying to perform well enough for him. They can't. He created people to have a relationship with him, to enjoy his love. But humanity rejected God and severed that relationship. His program is putting it back together."

He paused, took a bite, then gestured with his fork toward me. "Let me ask you this. When Sara is seven and she does something wrong, how many dishes will she have to wash before she can sit in your lap and have you hug her again?"

"None."

"How many A's will she have to make in school?"

"That's ridiculous."

"Why?"

"She won't have to do anything. She's my daughter."

"Exactly."

I looked down and sampled some more of my salad, letting that sink in. Finally my gaze returned to him. "You're saying that we can't do anything to earn God's acceptance."

He smiled and reached for the wine bottle. "A little more?"

"Sure."

He poured me half a glass. My mind was still racing from his last statement—or my summation. He proceeded.

"Muslims who try to earn their way into paradise—how many daily prayers do they have to perform to be good enough?"

"I don't know."

"Neither do they. That's the problem. They can never be sure if they've done enough—enough praying, fasting, giving to the poor, making pilgrimages. They can never know. Ask them, and they will admit that. Hindus can never know how many hundreds of lifetimes it may take to successfully work out their karma. Buddhists can never know how much effort it will take to reach nirvana."

"But Christianity is no different," I responded. "No one can ever know if he has really been good enough to make it to heaven."

"Oh, people can know that for certain. The answer is, they haven't been. No one is good enough to make it to heaven. No one can ever be good enough, no matter how hard they try."

"But what about all the people who think that going to church or giving money or being a good person will get them into heaven? Mrs. Willard, my Sunday school teacher, sure thought that would get people in."

"She was wrong. It won't."

This was stretching my concept of Christianity. "So you're saying that doing all the right things, like keeping the Ten Commandments, won't get you into heaven?"

"Correct."

"Then why do them?"

"There's great profit in obeying God. It just won't get you into heaven."

For a moment I didn't know what to say. *How can this guy say something so different from what I heard in church growing up?* Maybe he realized my predicament, because he resumed the conversation.

"You're a *Star Trek* fan."

I didn't know where he got his information, and I had decided to stop asking. "I liked *The Next Generation.* I never got into the follow-ups much."

"There's an episode where they talk about a rift, a tear, in the fabric of space-time. It's a huge problem. The galaxy will be destroyed if they don't repair it."

"Something tells me we're not going to start talking about *Star Trek.*"

"Maybe not," he replied. "But it's a great illustration. There is a moral fabric to the universe. Humanity's rebellion against God is a massive rip in that fabric. It's an overthrow of the entire way God designed the universe to operate. Every person's sin tears this moral fabric."

It was hard to deny that humanity is pretty screwed up. The evening news proved that.

"But who is to say that humanity isn't evolving spiritually? Like Dave and Paula say, maybe we're all moving toward a greater universal harmony." I had to admit I wasn't too convinced myself, but it was worth considering. Momentarily, at least.

"Humanity's separation from God is much more profound than people realize. Just look around. The selfishness, bitterness, hatred, prejudice, exploitation, abuse, wars—all these result from humanity's rebellion against God. Do you think God designed people to operate this way?"

"But some of those things are getting better," I chimed in optimistically.

"Really?" His eyebrows rose. "How many people were murdered by their own governments in the last century?"

"Oh, I dunno," I replied. "A hundred million or so."

"And how many killed in wars?"

"Probably about the same."

"In what century have the most people been killed for their faith?"

"Let me guess. The last one?"

"Right. And in what century do you think there has been more ecological damage, exploitation of the world's poor, rampant immorality—"

"Okay, you've made your point," I said, halting the litany of human ills.

"There's a rip in the fabric of the universe," he repeated. "God stands on one side of the tear; you stand on the other. And there's no way for you to repair it. There's no way at all to the other side. Trying to be good enough is irrelevant. Humanity rejected God, separated itself from him, and can't do anything to reestablish that relationship."

"Why not?"

"Because only God is big enough to fix the tear."

I had a feeling he was going to say that.

6

The Main Course

THE PROBLEM WITH places like Milano's is that by the time the main course arrives, you're stuffed. Well, not completely stuffed, but at a point where you wouldn't consider ordering veal fantarella with grilled vegetables. Of course, when the veal comes, and you take your first bite, room magically reappears in your belly.

I had been stuffed with God talk years ago, and I still felt the need for a good purge. But here I was, forty minutes into this dinner, and I hadn't reached my fill. I'm not sure why. To be honest, this guy both intrigued and baffled me. There he sat, one minute eating his salmon as if this dinner was the most natural thing in the world, the next saying stuff about God I'm certain I never heard in Sunday school.

"Do you have something to write on?" He took a pen from his coat pocket.

I pulled out my wallet and searched through it. "Not really. A couple of receipts. A business card."

"That'll do."

I turned it to the blank side and handed it to him. He continued. "Who is the best person you can think of?"

"What do you mean?"

"Morally speaking. Who is the best?"

"I don't know." I thought for a moment. "Living or dead?"

"Either."

"Mother Teresa maybe. She had a fairly good reputation."

"Okay." He drew a short line near the top of the card and put "Mother Teresa" next to it. "Who is the worst?"

"Well, Osama bin Laden turned out pretty bad, but there have been worse. Hitler. Stalin. Pol Pot."

"Pick one."

"Hitler."

He marked a line near the bottom and wrote "Hitler" next to it. Turning the card around toward me, he offered me the pen. I took it from him. "Now, Mother Teresa is at the top. Hitler is at the bottom. Where do you think you fall on this scale?"

The busboy appeared behind my companion and filled his water glass. I let the conversation pause while he came around and filled mine. He left, and I returned to the question at hand. "How can anyone answer that? If you put yourself closer to Mother Teresa, you look vain. If you put yourself closer to Hitler..." I let that speak for itself.

"So where do you think?" he asked, unmoved by my dilemma.

I raised the pen. "Here." I drew a mark above the middle, somewhat closer to Mother Teresa. "So what do I win?"

"Nothing. But I will tell you how you stack up in God's eyes."

"Okay." At least, that's what I said. I wasn't really sure I wanted to hear my score.

"Actually, this business card doesn't constitute the entire scale. Hitler is here." He pointed at the bottom. "You say you are here, and Mother Teresa is here. But to get a feel for how high God's actual standard is"—he stood the card on its end—"imagine that we went to Chicago and put this card at the base of the Sears Tower. God's moral standard is the top of the tower, over one hundred stories up."

"Are you saying that to God, Mother Teresa and Hitler are essentially the same?"

"Oh no. Hitler was horribly evil. Mother Teresa did very much good. It is not the same. But the point is this: Mother Teresa, in her own goodness, is no closer to bridging the gap to God than Hitler is. They are both sinners, and both on their own merits are separated from God."

I thought about that for a few seconds before responding. "So you're saying that no one can make it."

"Not on their own merit. No one is even close. God's standard is perfection. And you wouldn't want it any other way."

I was still thinking about the implications of his prior statement; this new one took a second to register. "I'm sorry. What? What do you mean, I wouldn't want it any other way?"

"You wouldn't want the universe run by someone who wasn't perfectly holy and perfectly just."

"Why not?" *Perfect holiness is the last thing I need to deal with.*

"Because it would offend your God-given sense of justice. Would you want a universe where crime went unpunished? Where, if someone harmed Sara, there'd be no justice? Where evil reigned unopposed? God has to punish sin, because if he doesn't, he lets all creation be sabotaged. How would it have been if, after the Holocaust, God had said to Hitler, 'That's okay, Adolf. We all make mistakes. Don't worry about it'?"

"But everyone isn't Hitler!"

"No, but everyone is a rebel against God. It doesn't take horrific outward acts. For the universe, humanity's rebellion is more like cancer than like a heart attack. It isn't mass murder that destroys the world. It's selfishness, resentment, envy, pride—all the daily sins of the heart. God has to deal with the cancer."

"But we've all felt those things. We're human."

"Yes."

I waited for more, but he returned to his salmon. The import of what he had said slowly sank in. "It just doesn't seem right that God sees everyone the same way. Some people are worse than others."

"And God will judge them all rightly. But that's the point. Everyone is already under God's judgment, because everyone has violated his moral law. On what basis are you going to stand before a perfectly holy God and say that you've been good enough?"

I picked up my fork to stab another piece of veal, then put it down again and reached for some water. Suddenly the conversation unsettled me.

"You read *Lord of the Flies,*" he resumed, "about the shipwrecked English boys who created their own society and ended up brutalizing each other."

"Yeah."

"Why did they come to accept such brutality as normal?"

"They were cut off from civilization. I suppose they gradually forgot what was right. At least, it got all mixed up for them."

He nodded. "It did. They lacked a compass to guide their behavior. Humanity is the same way. People are cut off from God, so they've lost a sense of how abhorrent sin really is. They live in a sinful world, and it almost seems normal. But to God it is grotesque. God is holy and just, in an absolute sense. Humanity doesn't have any point of comparison with that. That's why people continually try to water down God's holiness. The way Islam does."

My ears perked up on that one. "Like Islam? If there's one thing Muslims emphasize, it's God's justice and his punishment of wickedness."

"That's what they claim. But ask them what happens on the judgment day. They say that if you've done enough good deeds, Allah will overlook your bad ones, and you'll get into paradise."

"So?"

"So Allah has to deny perfect justice in order to be merciful. There's no penalty for wrongdoing if you have done enough good things to offset it. But true justice doesn't work that way, not even on earth. If someone is convicted of fraud, the judge doesn't say, 'Well, he was a kind Little League coach. That offsets it.' In Islam, Allah is not perfectly just, because if he were, people would have to pay the penalty for every sin, and no one would get into paradise. That's what perfect justice is."

I pushed the vegetables around on my neglected plate. "But I thought God is forgiving. You're implying that because of justice, God can't forgive."

"God is forgiving. God wants to forgive people more than anything in the world, to restore them to himself. What I'm saying is that God's desire to forgive doesn't negate his perfect justice. Someone has to pay the penalty for sins. God's justice demands it."

This seemed like a Catch-22 of the worst kind. I reached for a piece of bread, mostly to buy time to think. He finished off his salmon, apparently content to let me formulate my next question.

"So what has to happen to get us back to God?"

"God had two options. He could let people pay for their own sins..."

"Resulting in..."

"Humanity being separated from him forever."

"That's not a good one. What was the other option?"

"Or God could pay the penalty himself."

"How?"

"He is God. The Creator is greater than the creation. For the Creator to take the penalty of death himself, instead of those he created, satisfies perfect justice."

"Why would God do that?"

He reached for his water. "Let me ask you something.

Imagine that Sara is seventeen, and she falls in with a bad crowd and gets hooked on heroin."

"That's a little bleak, don't you think?"

"Just hypothetically. Now, if while on drugs, she murdered someone and was sentenced to death, would you take her penalty if you could?"

That was a hard one. Needless to say, I hadn't exactly pondered it before. But…

"I'm sure I would."

"Why?"

"Because I love her. And she would have the rest of her life, and I would want to give her the chance to make it a good one."

He leaned toward me, moved his plate forward, and rested his forearms against the table. "Don't you think God loves you at least as much as you love Sara?"

I shifted back in my chair, but my eyes never left his. "Maybe. I really don't know."

He leaned back himself. "I heard about two boys in fifth grade. One of them made straight A's; the other barely passed every year. Despite their different grades, they were best friends—had been since kindergarten.

"Near the end of the school year, they had a big math test. The first boy sailed through it; the second, who needed to make a C to pass, struggled. After class, the first asked the second how he did. 'I don't think I made it,' he said. That day at recess, while everyone played outside, the first boy sneaked back into the classroom, shuffled through the stack of tests, and found their two. He erased his name on his and wrote his friend's name there and then wrote his name on his friend's."

I waited for a second, but he seemed to be finished. "That's all?"

"What else were you expecting?"

"Well, the story's not over. When the teacher returned and graded the papers, she would have known what he did."

"No. The story ends there. What does it tell you?"

"That the first kid was willing to exchange his grade so that his friend could pass."

"Yes, and more than that." He ran his hand across his chin. "What would have happened if the second kid had failed?"

"He would have been held back the next year probably."

"And then…"

"They couldn't have gone through school together anymore."

He paused for a moment, then spoke a little more softly. "God longs to have you with him. That's why he created you. But your sin separates you from him. It has to, if God is just. You have to be innocent before God. So, to get you back,

God took your sin upon himself, and he died to pay for it. That satisfies his justice. In exchange, he offers you a not-guilty verdict. He offers it as a free gift."

I wasn't entirely sure about this alleged gift, which sounded too good to be true, but I had to ask the logical question. "What do you have to do to get it?"

"Just receive it. That's all."

"You don't have to do anything for it?"

"No."

"And how do you receive it?"

"Just trust him. That's what all relationships are built on: trust. You reestablish a relationship with God by trusting that he died to pay for your sins. Believe that he will forgive your sins and give you eternal life. That's why he died for you. He wants you back. All you have to do is accept the gift."

I wanted to look away, but my eyes seemed frozen. I wasn't convinced that God loved me all that much, and I sure didn't know if I wanted him. And this last statement confused me.

"I don't get it. The Bible says that Jesus died on the cross, not God."

"Nick," he replied, "I am God."

7

The Dessert

"EXCUSE ME A minute, would you?"

I stood and headed toward the men's room. Passing the lattice, I hooked a right and entered the bathroom. I took care of business, stepped to the sink, and looked at myself in the mirror.

Now what?

It's not every day that someone tells you he's God. Maybe if you worked in a psych ward—I don't know.

This guy is either a nut or a really good actor or...

I dismissed the last possibility. *But why would anyone want to put on this show? What would be the point—to bamboozle me "into the kingdom"? Who would do that? Okay, I can think of a few televangelists who might, but this guy doesn't come off that way. I can't refute anything he's said. I don't necessarily agree with it all, but it's not off the wall. Except that last statement.*

I splashed my face with water, dried off, and headed back toward the table, unsure what to do. I considered taking a right at the lattice and going straight for the parking lot, but something stopped me. I couldn't help wanting to know more about this guy who claimed to be…

I returned to the table. Our plates had been replaced by dessert menus.

"The waiter recommends the strawberry amaretto cake."

He looked over his menu. I stared at him, waiting for him to put it down and look up at me. He finally did.

"Prove it."

"Prove…"

"That you're God."

"What would convince you?"

Good question. What could anyone possibly do to convince you of that?

"You couldn't even turn wine into water earlier."

"That's your assumption."

"What?! Are you saying you could have but just chose not to?"

"And what if I had changed it?"

"Well, it might have gotten my attention."

"And then what?"

Another good question. It's not like he doesn't have my attention sufficiently.

The waiter interrupted with a request for dessert selections. I motioned across the table and glanced at the menu. I couldn't concentrate. My host ordered the cake.

"And for you, sir?"

"The tiramisu." An old standby.

I watched him collect the menus and walk off. My host resumed the conversation. "You're having a hard time believing that God would become a man."

"Well," I half chuckled, half snorted, "wouldn't you?"

"Maybe. It depends on what I expected from God."

"I don't expect him to look as if he just finished the day at Merrill Lynch."

He laughed gently. "No, I wouldn't either, I suppose."

I leaned back and folded my arms. "And to be honest, I really don't believe that God asks people just to take a blind leap of faith about him."

"You're right. He doesn't. That's what the world's religions do."

"What's the difference between them and what you're saying?"

"About one hundred eighty degrees. In this case God gives proof before he expects faith. But the world's religions have no evidence for their claims. Various forms of Hinduism count over three hundred million gods. What proof do they have of their existence?"

"None, as far as I'm concerned."

He motioned his index finger toward me. "That's why you're not a Hindu. You see no reason to believe it. What evidence can Buddhists offer that ultimate reality is an unknowable void called nirvana? Who can demonstrate to you that God actually spoke to Muhammad? Or to Joseph Smith of the Mormons? Or—"

"But Jesus is just the same. What evidence is there that Jesus was God?" I noticed that my elbows had migrated onto the table.

"Well, for one thing, that's exactly what God said would happen."

"When did he say that?"

He took a drink of water before continuing. "You've read some of the prophets."

"I never paid much attention to that Nostradamus stuff."

His brow furrowed. "The real ones," he insisted.

I had, in fact, read some of the Hebrew prophets. Elizabeth, my girlfriend back at NIU, had successfully goaded me into attending a dorm Bible study that covered them.

"They said the Messiah would come," I answered. "I don't think they ever said anything about his being God."

"You focused more on Elizabeth at that study than on the Bible. I suggest you reread Isaiah, Daniel, and Micah."

"How did you know—"

"I was there."

I looked intently at him for several moments. He kept his eyes on mine, but I couldn't read his expression. I ignored his last comment. "I know what they wrote. They said the Messiah would be born of a virgin, born in Bethlehem. They described his crucifixion, et cetera, et cetera."

"That's a pretty good tip-off, don't you think? Micah predicting seven centuries in advance the village where the Messiah would be born? David describing in detail death by crucifixion, centuries before the Romans invented the practice? Daniel telling the year of the Messiah's death, five hundred years ahead of time?"

"Really?" I was genuinely surprised. "What year?"

"Calculating by the Jewish calendar, AD 33."

I wasn't sure what to say to that. I emptied my wineglass.

He continued. "As for saying the Messiah would be God himself, the prophets said that he would be called Mighty God, Eternal Father, that he would be from days of eternity, that he would be worshiped."

That did sound eerily divine, but I wasn't about to admit it. "Still, that doesn't mean Jesus was God. Did you see that two-night miniseries they did on Jesus?"

"I know the one you're talking about."

"And that show Peter Jennings did awhile back on the historical Jesus?"

"Not particularly accurate."

"You say that, but how do we know? It portrayed Jesus as someone who never claimed to be the Messiah, much less God. It said he struggled with his identity, got swept up in events, and was killed as a political threat."

He answered matter-of-factly. "I forgave sins on my own authority, healed people, raised people from the dead, exercised power over nature, said I existed before Abraham, claimed to be one with the Father, said I was the giver of eternal life, and accepted worship. Who does that sound like to you?"

"Just because you claimed to be God doesn't mean that you are."

"No. But it does mean that I wasn't just a good religious teacher. Either I told the truth about who I am, or I lied, or I was insane. Those are the only real options. Good religious teachers don't claim to be God."

He looked off across the room, not seeming to focus on anything in particular. He shook his head almost imperceptibly, then looked back at me. "People distort the truth because they reject the final proof I've already given."

"What's that?"

"That I rose from the dead."

At that moment the waiter, easily within earshot of our

last exchange, appeared with our desserts. I avoided his eyes as he served them, refilled our water, and then departed. I spoke first.

"You're sitting here—alive—across the table from me. If you say you were once dead, it's pretty hard for me to prove otherwise."

He took a bite of a strawberry. "Good point. Why don't we deal with the actual facts? What do you know about me historically?"

His use of the first person still disconcerted me, but I could go for this topic. I plunged in. "From secular histories, we know Jesus was an actual person."

"Okay."

"We know he was a teacher who had a large following."

He nodded.

"We know the Romans executed him," I continued.

"Which brings us to the event in question. What happened then?"

"Well, his disciples claimed that he was raised from the dead, but of course they would claim that."

"Really? Is that what they expected to happen?"

I searched through my Sunday school data bank. "Not that I recall," I admitted.

"Despite the fact that I told them repeatedly it would."

"True."

"Did they believe it at first, when the women told them about it?"

"No."

"When did they believe?"

"According to their accounts, when they actually saw Jesus."

"So when these men wrote accounts of my life, they describe themselves as failing to believe beforehand, failing to believe afterward, and only believing after they were hit in the face with the evidence, and even then they stayed in hiding, afraid of the authorities. Is that the way you would portray yourself if you wanted people to follow you in a cause?"

"It's possible," I answered. *Improbable, perhaps, but possible.*

"For what purpose?" He lifted a fork to his cake. "So they could be impoverished, persecuted, and finally martyred?"

"Lots of people have died for believing something false."

"Yes, for a false philosophy or false religious belief. But this is different. We're talking about people who willingly died for their belief in a historical event. They were there. They saw whether it happened. They all said it happened, even though saying so brought them nothing but suffering and death. People don't die for something they know is a lie, especially when it brings them no benefit."

High-school debate had taught me a thing or two about argumentation. Like when to drop a losing point. I sampled my tiramisu and thought a moment. "Maybe they thought Jesus had died, when he really hadn't."

"How often do you think the Romans let people who had not yet died down off crosses?"

"Probably not too often."

"So you're implying the Romans let someone down so badly injured as to be left for dead, then two days later my recovery was so miraculous that the disciples thought I was God himself?"

"Okay, it's unlikely," I replied. "But the disciples did have something to gain from claiming Jesus had been resurrected."

"Go on."

"They had status to gain as those who began a new religious movement."

His answer surprised me. "You're right. They did have that status." He leaned forward and rested his fork on his dessert plate. "You're saying that the men who spread the word about me, who taught people to love one another, who told slave owners in a brutal society to treat their slaves well, who told husbands to love their wives at a time when women were treated as chattel, who told people to honor and obey the government that was martyring them, who launched the greatest force for good that the world has known, that they did all this based on something they knew to be false?"

"It hasn't all been good," I retorted. "What about the Crusades? Or the Salem witch trials? Or the Spanish Inquisition? What about Europe's Wars of Religion between the Protestants and the Catholics, or the fighting in Northern Ireland? Your own people are always at each other's throats."

His countenance changed noticeably, and he let out an audible sigh. "That's true." He remained silent for a few moments, looking at the table. "It makes me very sad."

The change in him disarmed me, taking me off the defensive and, frankly, off the offensive as well. I sat looking at him, then asked honestly, "Why has Christianity been such a mixed bag?"

He folded his hands on the table. "Several reasons. Most of the people who have done these things didn't really know me. They may have seemed outwardly religious, but they weren't mine. They never really put their trust in me."

"Pardon me for saying so, but that seems a little convenient for you."

"Not really. More than anything I wanted to have a relationship with them. But they wouldn't."

"Still," I countered, "you can't claim that no real Christians have perpetrated any of these things."

"No, I can't. That's the tragedy of it."

"It almost seems the norm."

He unfolded his hands and sat back. "It isn't. But it's been too frequent."

"Why?"

"Because they never learned to live as the new people they were."

"I'm not sure what you mean."

"When people put their trust in me and receive eternal life, they get more than forgiveness. Otherwise, heaven would be populated with a bunch of forgiven sinners still running from God. God won't have that."

"So what does he do about it?"

"He does more than forgive them. He changes them on the inside. Their heart, their human spirit, is actually made new. In the depths of their being they no longer run from God; they are joined to him. They no longer want to disobey God; they want to do what he says is good."

"But they don't do it," I objected.

"Often they do. But not always. A new heart gets you in the game. Then you have to let me be your instructor. I teach you how to live based on what's been made new on the inside. Some people don't let me do that. They'd rather do it their way. So they remain judgmental or selfish or fearful. There's no joy in that."

"This sounds almost New Agey, like something Dave and Paula would say."

"Maybe," he answered, "but it's not. Tell me, you've talked to your two friends enough. What do you think they're after?"

"Connection with the divine, I suppose. Except they believe they already are divine in a sense. It's a little confusing."

He nodded as he finished a bite of cake. "How do they try to connect with God?"

"More enlightenment," I replied, more as a question than as a statement. "Working on letting go of misguided desires and embracing"—my New Age vocabulary was failing me—"embracing something. I'm not sure what."

"They're trying to achieve through a lot of effort the very thing I offer for free."

"What's that?"

"When someone receives me, God forgives them, he makes them new on the inside, and"—he paused momentarily—"he comes to live in them."

I had been downing my tiramisu during his explanation, but this last statement caused me to halt an approaching bite. "He what?"

"He comes to live in them. That's as close to God as you can get. And unlike people trying to manufacture the connection on their own, it's the real thing."

I wasn't sure that sounded like a great deal. "The last thing I need is God looking over my shoulder every minute."

"He's already looking over your shoulder every minute. What you need is him living in you every minute."

"What for?"

"Well, for one, how else are you ever going to love your daughter unconditionally, to say nothing of Mattie? You want to love Mattie better, but you don't know how. And even if you did know, you don't have the ability. Only God loves that way. He wants to do it through you."

He was right. Despite my best intentions, things weren't going all that well with Mattie. I constantly found myself getting irritated with her, and she with me. I was afraid Nick the romancer had gone into hibernation. I picked up my fork, took a bite of tiramisu, and finally spoke. "I've never heard all this before."

"I know. My disciples knew it and lived it and passed it on. But the message got distorted along the way. Church hierarchies, power structures—they crowded it out. People wanted to reduce God to a set of rules. But he's not about rules, any more than marriage is about rules."

"Then what's he about?"

"Joining people to himself. He designed them to be joined to him, like man and woman are made to be united. People were meant to have God's very life in them. Without that, they're like a new SUV with no engine. They may look good, but they don't work. They're missing the most important part."

I leaned back to take in what he'd said. "If this is what Christianity is all about, why don't they say it?"

"Because most haven't understood. Some have, though. It's never been hidden. Read the last third of John's gospel. It's all there. Mr. McIntosh knew it."

"My seventh-grade science teacher. I always liked him."

"Believe it or not, he liked you too."

"All the times he sent me to detention?"

He smiled. "You didn't give him much choice, did you?"

"No." I smiled back. "I suppose I didn't."

I took another bite of my dessert, as did he. We sat silently for a couple of minutes as I cleaned my plate. I finally broke the silence.

"So. Where do we go from here?"

"That's a good question," he said. "Where do you want to go?"

I wasn't sure.

8

The Coffee

"WHY DOESN'T GOD just show himself to people?"

The waiter had walked off with our dessert plates. I had resisted the urge to scrape mine with my fork as I usually did at home. Waiting for coffee, I decided it was now or never to get some of my remaining questions about God and life answered. This one seemed like a decent place to start.

Jesus wiped his mouth with his napkin and returned it to his lap. "What would you have me do?"

"I don't know—appear to everyone personally."

He chuckled, and seeing the irony in my statement, I couldn't help but join him momentarily.

"No, seriously," I said. "Most people don't get a dinner invitation."

"I did appear to humanity. I became one of you. That's about as personal as it gets."

"But that was two thousand years ago."

"It doesn't matter. Most people didn't believe then, either. You don't have to see with your eyes to believe."

I rested an elbow on the back of my chair. "At least God could perform some kind of sign that would show he exists."

"I did that, too. They still didn't believe. My Father did that at Mount Sinai with the Jews. They turned away from him within six weeks."

The waiter appeared with our coffee orders: a cappuccino for me, regular coffee for him. He used a little cream, no sugar.

"It's not a matter of further visual evidence," he continued. "People have all the evidence they need. It's a matter of the heart. Do they want to trust God and humbly receive the gift he offers, or do they insist on proving themselves good enough and doing it their own way?"

Somehow his statements about "people" seemed to have a very personal application. I wanted to keep the conversation on a more impersonal level.

"But how can you say people have all the evidence they need?"

"They have creation to tell them that God exists. Humanity knows more than ever before how intricately designed and finely tuned creation is. People have me to tell them what God is like. That's one reason I came, to reveal the Father. They have my resurrection to prove I am God. They have the Bible as God's message to them."

I took my first sip of cappuccino, licking the foam off my lips as he drank some coffee. "My religion professor said so many copying errors were made over the years that we don't really know what the original Bible said."

He shook his head slightly as he put his cup down. "He doesn't do much research, does he? As I said before, he would find the opposite is true. It's been painstakingly copied. The number of places where you have a question of any consequence is minuscule."

I had to admit I hadn't done the research, either. I forged ahead. "But what about all the contradictions?"

"Like what?"

"I don't know. Like...I don't know specifics. I just know there are supposed to be contradictions."

He smiled. "I'll give you one. One gospel account says I healed two blind men outside of Jericho. Another says I healed one."

"There you go."

"Okay. The other day when you told Les that you and Mattie had gone to a movie, had the two of you gone alone?"

"No, Mattie's friend Jessica came with us."

"Why did you leave that fact out?"

"It wasn't relevant to the story I was telling."

"True."

I expected more, but he stopped there.

"Are you saying the Bible's historical accounts are true?"

"Your own archaeologists are telling you that. You should have renewed your subscription to *U.S. News & World Report.* Check out a cover story on it."

"But I can't believe that God really created the universe in six days or that the earth is only six thousand years old. That's preposterous."

"Who is asking you to believe that?"

"All those fundamentalists. They added up all the genealogies in Genesis and said that the earth was created six thousand years ago."

He took another sip of coffee. "Genesis presents a flow of history. It says that God created the universe in an orderly fashion, starting with light itself. He made the earth, then gave it design: forming continents out of the oceans, creating plant life, creating animal life, creating humanity in his image. Now, is there anything in that sequence that your scientists would disagree with?"

"Well, they wouldn't agree with the 'in God's image' part."

"No. That's their problem isn't it? They don't want to acknowledge that they are created in God's image, because that would make them accountable to a Creator. They don't want that."

"But what about all the miracles? Like Joshua marching

around Jericho seven days, then the walls falling. Or David plunking Goliath in the middle of the forehead. Or God parting the Red Sea."

"Are you implying that the Creator of the universe can't perform miracles?"

"You wouldn't even change my wine back into water." I was unable to restrain a slight smirk.

He returned to the miracles. "I'll grant you, David and Goliath would be hard to verify outside the Bible. But they've already discovered the ruins of Jericho. The city was built just as the Bible describes it. And the walls fell in exactly the manner described too."

"You're kidding."

"No. As for the Red Sea, give your archaeologists a couple of decades." He winked. "But that's not the real issue, is it?" He put down his coffee and leaned forward. "Remember how, when you were six, you couldn't believe a two-wheeled bike would stay upright under you, until you tried it and you saw that it would?"

"Sure."

"If you actually open up the Bible and ask God to speak to you, Nick, you'll see that he will."

We looked into one another's eyes a moment. I finally spoke again. "Not everyone has access to a Bible."

"No," he acknowledged, "not everyone does."

"So what does God do about them?"

"The Father asks people to respond to the revelation they've been given. That may only be creation and their conscience. That's what he holds them accountable for."

"But they never get to hear about you."

"If anyone is really willing to do what God asks, he will reveal himself to them."

I let out a disbelieving snort. "Well, if they don't have a Bible..."

"God can use whatever means he wishes. Usually he sends people. Sometimes in areas where the gospel is restricted, like in Muslim countries, I reveal myself in dreams."

"But it seems like people in some places have a huge advantage. They can hear about you all the time."

"Yes, and they ignore the message. As I said, God reveals himself to anyone willing to trust him. He provides his forgiveness to all who will accept it."

"And what about people who think they're good enough, like Mrs. Willard?"

"They will stand before God on their own merit." He lifted his cup to his lips once more, then returned it to the table. "That's not a position you want to be in. It's like a father who offers a billion-dollar inheritance to his son, but the son says to him, 'Not until I've proved myself worthy.' It seems noble to try to be good enough, but in reality it's just prideful obstinacy. The son wants the inheritance on his own terms. He doesn't want to accept it as a gift. But God offers it only as a gift. You can't earn it. No one can."

I took a long sip of my cappuccino, which had cooled some. This time I wiped off the foam with my napkin and placed it on the table instead of in my lap. I looked back up at him.

"Is there a hell?"

"Yes," he answered quietly. "For those who choose to stay separated from God, there is existence. It's not an existence you want."

I sat silently for a moment.

"What's it like?"

"If you remove all sources of good from life as you know it, that's what it's like. God is the source of all good. For those who choose separation from him, there is no good." He paused. "You can't even comprehend how bad that would be."

"Why does he send people there?"

"The Father offers forgiveness to anyone willing to receive him. People choose continued separation from God. He respects what they choose."

"But why doesn't he just make everyone go to heaven? They'd be happier there."

"Love doesn't force relationship," he said in a tone even softer than before. "If you had somehow forced Mattie to marry you, it wouldn't have been love. God created people to be able to choose freely. He honors their choices."

I thought about that for a moment. *Somehow it just doesn't seem ri—*

"You live in a world turned upside down by humanity's rebellion. Sometimes things don't make sense. When you don't let Sara play near the street, it doesn't make sense to her. One day it will. God loves with a love greater than you can know. He doesn't want anyone separated from him. But some will be. One day that will make sense."

"I don't find that answer entirely satisfying."

"I know," he replied. "That's okay."

I took another drink and gathered my thoughts. "I suppose you'll say that God allowing suffering is the same kind of thing."

"What do you think?"

"Based on what you've said, humanity suffers because it separated itself from God."

"Yes."

"So why doesn't he just make things right, right now? Why wait for some day in the future?"

He drank some coffee. "That's difficult to answer, because you can't see things from God's perspective right now. But there is a purpose to the present time. And one day everything will be made right."

"That doesn't quite seem fair, for God to work out his plan while we suffer."

"You're forgetting something. God didn't leave you to suffer alone. He suffered more than anyone."

I looked down at my cappuccino for a few moments. The foam had flattened out, and it was only lukewarm. I took a couple of sips, lost in my thoughts. Finally he spoke.

"You're angry about your dad."

"God took him away when I was sixteen. I'd say that's worth being mad about. Or was that just part of God's plan?" My voice was rising, and I glanced around to see if anyone had overheard me. *Oh, who cares?* I turned back to Jesus.

He sat silently, his eyes held on mine. "You loved your dad very much."

I glanced back at my cup and eventually spoke toward it. "We used to do a lot together—go fishing, go to Cub games, Blackhawk games. He had played some semipro hockey for a while, and he coached all my hockey teams. After Mother divorced him and we moved across town, he stopped coaching me... I probably could have played college."

"You still saw him, though."

I figured that was a statement, not a question. I answered anyway. "Yeah. Every other weekend. But it wasn't the same."

"He missed you too." That was definitely a statement.

I finally looked up. "I know."

"You don't know how brokenhearted he was about you. It almost killed him to lose you."

"Well, he didn't live much longer anyway, did he?" I didn't even bother trying to hide my anger this time.

"No." He spoke quietly. "He didn't."

I drank the last of my cappuccino.

"This won't seem true to you," he said, "but I was heartbroken for both of you."

I put my cup down and stared across the table, not feeling anger so much as lifelessness. "You're right; that doesn't seem true."

We sat in silence.

"So," I finally said, "you never answered my question. Was my parents' divorce and my dad's death part of God's plan?"

He took a moment to reply. "You know the story of the prodigal son."

"Yeah." *Great. Another Sunday school lesson.*

"What did it take for the son to return to the father, who loved him?"

I answered in a monotone, listless voice. "For life to get really bad, in the pigpen. So what?"

"Sometimes…it takes deep hurts for people to feel their need for God."

"And that's God's plan?"

"That's what God is willing to use in a broken world. Your dad's pain drove him to me. And without that wound in your heart, Nick, you wouldn't be sitting here talking with me, either."

I leaned back, folded my arms, and sighed. "I wish I could say it all makes sense now." I looked aside momentarily, then back at him. "I wish I could say that."

9

The Bill

THE RESTAURANT HAD emptied. I glanced around to where the table of six had laughed the evening away. It was reset for tomorrow's lunch. The young couple had long since left. Even a middle-aged pair in the corner who had entered during our entrée had departed. *Have we been talking that long?*

The place had the eerie quiet that comes when your party closes down a restaurant for the night. I could hear the *clink* of someone sorting utensils. Our waiter approached our table.

"Another cappuccino, sir?" he asked me.

"No, this was fine."

He looked toward Jesus. "And you, sir? More coffee?"

"No, thank you. We're ready for the bill."

"Yes, sir."

My eyes followed as he stepped toward the front of the restaurant. Turning back to the table, I saw Jesus loosening his tie for the first time.

"Even I don't like these things," he said.

God doesn't like neckties. Note that for future reference.

The waiter reappeared with a black leather bill holder and placed it on the table between us. He then turned to Jesus, held out a blank piece of paper and a pen, and in a hushed voice said, "Can I have your autograph, sir? Just in case."

Jesus smiled and took the pen and paper. "Of course." He wrote more than his name (I couldn't tell what) and handed it back to the waiter. *I wonder how much that'll go for on eBay.*

"Thank you very much, sir."

"Thank you, Eduardo," he replied.

Their eyes stayed on one another as they held the paper between them, then Eduardo took it, paused, and walked away.

For the first time since the meal began, I regarded my host. His features remained the same—the dark hair, the olive complexion, the almost black eyes, the toned muscles—but somehow his look had changed. He seemed at the same time softer and yet more authoritative. I wasn't entirely comfortable with him, yet I was strangely drawn to him.

Jesus turned back to me. "I like Eduardo. He's a humble man."

The longer we'd talked, the more questions had popped

into my mind. What was the universe like before the Big Bang? Is there intelligent life on other planets? What really happened to the dinosaurs? But with the bill on the table, one question overshadowed the others.

"You keep telling me that God offers me this free gift, eternal life. So what's heaven like?"

He smiled as if I had asked about his hometown. "Heaven is a cool place. Humanity's senses have been so dulled by living in this broken world, you wouldn't believe all the sights, sounds, smells. Colors you've never seen. Music you've never heard. Lots of activity, yet overwhelming peacefulness. Remember how you felt when you stood at the Grand Canyon—too awestruck to take it all in?"

"Yeah."

"Heaven is like that, only infinitely more."

"I feel stupid asking this, but are the streets really made of gold?"

He laughed. "Describing heaven isn't exactly easy. It's like explaining snow to a tribal native from the Amazon. He doesn't have a point of reference for it. What's written in the Bible is true, but in a way greater than you can imagine."

"And you're saying I don't have to do anything to get there?"

"You have to receive the gift of eternal life," he answered. "You can't trust in your own goodness. You have to put your faith in me." He shifted to the side and took a long drink of water, then put the glass down. "But you're confusing heaven and eternal life."

My mind was still partly on what heaven might look like, so I didn't quite take in his last statement. "What? I'm sorry."

"You're confusing heaven and eternal life."

"I thought they were the same thing."

"No."

"I'm not following you."

"Eternal life isn't a place," he responded. "And it's not primarily length of existence. I am eternal life. The Father is eternal life."

"I'm not sure I'm getting what you're saying."

"Just as God is the source of all physical life, he is also the source of all spiritual life. Think of it this way. God created your body to need food, air, and water. What happens when you remove those things?"

"You die."

"The same thing holds true for your spirit. God created your spirit to be joined with him. Without him, it's dead. It has no life. God is spirit, and he is life. The only way for you to have eternal life is to have him."

I still wasn't sure I was connecting all the dots. "So when you say God offers eternal life..."

"He is offering you himself. God comes to live within you forever. When you have me, you have Life itself. With a capital L."

I leaned back and thought that over for a moment. "So what is heaven?"

"Heaven is simply a place where I am."

"But people don't go to heaven until they die."

"True. But you can have eternal life right now."

I must have had a confused look on my face again.

"Eternal life isn't something that starts when you die," he continued. "It's something that starts the minute you receive me. When you put your trust in me, you are not only completely forgiven, but I also join myself to your spirit. I come to live within you."

"You? Sitting right there?"

"The Holy Spirit, if you wish. He and the Father and I are one."

"You know, I never really understood that whole Trinity thing. Father, Son, Holy Spirit…"

He smiled. "Join the crowd. You aren't meant to understand it."

"Are you saying I'm incapable of understanding it?"

"Yes."

I wasn't sure how to respond.

"God wouldn't be much of a God," he said, "if you could fully understand his nature. Humanity still hasn't figured out most of creation. The Creator is far greater than that."

The significance of what he'd been saying was slowly dawning on me. I didn't fully comprehend it, but I got the gist of it. I just wasn't sure about the implications. "I'm still not entirely comfortable with God coming to live in me. I like the forgiveness part. But this other—"

"Is the best part. You need someone to love you and accept you and want to be with you, even when you feel bad about yourself. Someone who will always be with you. Everyone needs that. God made you that way."

"Sara wants to be around me," I half joked.

"Wait till she's fifteen."

That seems ages away.

"And," he said, "to tell you the truth, you need someone to put some adventure back in your life. Remember the kid who used to go dirt biking on Highback Ridge?"

I felt a spark of energy at the mention of the place. "Several times I almost didn't make it off there."

"I know." A smile edged onto his face. "You were quite a daredevil."

He leaned forward, resting his forearms on the table. "You're bored, Nick. You were made for more than this. You're worried about God stealing your fun, but you've got it backward. You're like a kid who doesn't want to leave for Disney World because he's having fun making mud pies by the curb. He doesn't realize that what's being offered is so much better. There's no adventure like being joined to the Creator of the universe." He leaned back from the table. "And your first mission would be to let him guide you out of the mess you're in at work."

My expression froze, and my eyes locked on his. Two months earlier I had discovered that the company was fabricating data on its environmental testing results. I wasn't involved, but I knew enough to jeopardize my career if we were caught. *And he knows.*

"You want out," he said. "Why don't you leave?"

"But I can't quit. There aren't any jobs like mine in this area, and Mattie would kill me if we have to move again. She just got her graphics business back to where it was in Chicago."

"You know it cheats Mattie and Sara to have you working at Pruitt. Not only are you risking your career, it's draining you. You're not there for them."

I stared across the table at him. Just talking about this drained me. *He's right. But...*

"I just can't do that, not now."

"You need someone to give you strength to make that decision. Because it really will work out okay. I know it doesn't seem like it."

"That's the truth. Mattie would be furious. And then I'd be mad at her for reacting that way. And then…" *And then things would go downhill from there. For months.* This whole scenario was getting darker by the minute.

"What if someone lived in you who could love Mattie even when she's upset at you?"

That seems utterly impossible.

"It's not with God," he said.

"What?"

"Impossible. I can love her through you even when it's hardest for you. And in the day-to-day routine as well. She needs that."

I looked down to avoid his eyes. Talking about my work mess was bad enough; I certainly wasn't used to talking about this kind of stuff, especially with a guy. Even if he was Jesus. "I don't think God is exactly doing backflips over me."

He laughed, leaned back, and folded his hands behind his head. "You know one of the people I liked to hang around most when I was here before?"

I shook my head.

"I liked Nicodemus. He used to come and ask me questions. My answers always confounded him. But I liked seeing his eyes open to what we were talking about. He was a good man, but he held a seat on the ruling council, and they were dishonest with the people."

"Sounds like my kind of guy," I mumbled.

"You and he have more in common than just a name. In a good way, mostly."

He paused, glanced at the bill holder, then took a sip of water. As he did, I reached toward the bill. "Here, let me get this," I said. "I owe you one."

My hand grabbed the leather holder, but before I could move it, his hand landed on my wrist. I looked over at him.

"Nick, it's a gift."

I relaxed my grip on the leather and looked down toward his hand. Both his shirt and his suit jacket had slid slightly up his arm. My eyes locked on a large puncture scar on his wrist.

I stayed silent for a moment. "I thought they went through your hands."

He followed my eyes to the scar. "Most people think that. The stakes were nailed through the wrist to support the weight of my body. Hand tissue would tear apart if it had to hold the body up."

I let him have the check. He pulled two bills out of his front pocket, slid them inside the holder, and looked up at me.

"Are you ready?"

10

Home

We walked toward the front of the restaurant, past the lattice. *Funny, I almost bolted out this way awhile ago. Now I don't even want to leave.* I fell a pace or two behind, lost in my thoughts.

Did I really just have dinner with… Why me?… Does he do this all the time?… What am I going to tell Mattie?… When I wake up tomorrow… What do I do now?

I looked up and watched as Jesus conversed briefly with Carlo, who'd been sweeping the foyer. They hugged before Carlo opened the door for him. I followed. We paused under the awning.

"You and Carlo act like old friends."

"We are."

"How long have you been coming to Milano's?"

"This is my first time."

He took a step toward my car. We walked in silence across the parking lot. I should have guessed he would know which car was mine, but I wasn't yet accustomed to being with someone who knew everything. We stopped at the Explorer.

"Which car is yours?" I was curious to know which one God preferred.

"Oh, I didn't drive."

I let that one hang.

It felt a little uncomfortable at my car. How do you say good-bye to Jesus? He didn't seem uneasy, though.

"Thanks for dinner," I finally said. Suddenly an earlier question popped back into my mind. "You never told me who sent the invitation."

He chuckled a little but didn't respond.

"I suppose this was your idea from the start."

"Actually, it was yours, Nick. Do you remember when your dad left, and you asked God to come and tell you why?"

"Not really."

"Well, I remembered. I've been planning this dinner for a long time."

I wasn't sure what to say. I fumbled in my pocket for my keys, pulled them out, and unlocked the car. I wanted to tell him how glad I was that I had stayed and how the evening had turned out so differently than I had expected. He knew, I suppose, but I wanted to say it anyway. All that came out, though, was, "Will we get together for dinner again?"

He smiled gently. "That's up to you."

"I'm not sure what that means."

"Yes, you are. Hand me your other business card."

I pulled out my billfold and gave him my last one. He pulled his pen out of his coat pocket, wrote something on the back of the card, then slid it inside my shirt pocket.

"That'll tell you how to reach me."

He grasped the door handle and opened it. "Mattie is already asleep. You'd better get home."

I still had a thousand questions. But he was right. I climbed in the car, turned the key, and rolled my window down. Probably sensing my uncertainty, he initiated the farewell. "I'm glad you showed up, Nick. I've enjoyed our time."

"I have too."

"Remember: I'm for you. Mattie is too. She just hasn't learned to show it very well yet. Give her time. Love her."

"I will."

"Kiss Sara for me."

"I will."

I reached out my right hand to him. He took it and shook it firmly. I couldn't help glancing at the scar on his wrist once more. Reluctantly I pulled my hand back and put the Explorer in reverse.

"Good-bye," I said.

"Until next time," he replied.

I backed out, then started across the parking lot. Looking through the rearview mirror, I waved. But he was gone.

The drive home from Milano's takes about twenty minutes. It seemed to take two. My mind traveled a thousand times faster than the wheels did. I pulled into the driveway, cutting my lights early so as not to wake anyone. I killed the engine and, as I reached for my coat, remembered my business card that Jesus had written on. I slid it out of my pocket and turned it over. "Revelation 3:20" was all it said. *Revelation 3:20. A Bible verse? The book of Revelation?* I got out of the car and quietly shut the door.

The house was silent as I locked everything up. Mattie had left a single lamp on for me in the living room. Gretel raised her head as I passed by the kitchen. I stopped and gave her a pat. "Sorry you didn't get your walk tonight, girl," I whispered. She put her head back down, resuming her sleep. *I hope Mattie remembered to feed her.*

I tiptoed up the stairs and peeked into Sara's room. Sound asleep. I crept to the crib and gave her a good-night kiss. Her breathing altered slightly, then returned to its normal rhythm.

I turned around and walked down the hall to our bedroom. *I'm not sure what I'm getting myself into here.* Reaching across the bed, I closed a novel Mattie had fallen asleep reading.

"Hi," I whispered. "I'm home."

Mattie roused slightly, groaned a little, then cracked her eyes. "Hello, honey," she mumbled.

"I'm really sorry about tonight, Mattie—"

"I know. It's okay. Let's talk about it in the morning."

"Okay."

I kissed her and pulled the covers up to her head.

"I'll be here shortly."

"Okay," she said in a slight daze as she rolled over to sleep.

I went to the study, where I could undress without disturbing her. I found a hanger for my suit pants in the closet. Then I decided to look for something else. I crossed the room, closed the door, and returned to the closet, quietly pulling out boxes of books that we didn't have space to put on our bookshelves. I emptied three boxes, but no luck. *It's got to be here somewhere.* Piles of books littered the floor as I started my fourth box. *I am making a total mess.* Then, pay dirt. My old Bible. I hadn't opened it since college. *I'm surprised I even kept this thing.* I turned to the back where Revelation was, then glanced again at my business card. "3:20."

I turned to chapter 3. Verse 20 was on the next page. It was a quote from Jesus:

> Here I am! I stand at the door and knock;
> if anyone hears my voice and opens the door,
> I will come in to him and will dine with him,
> and he with me.

About the Author

David Gregory is the coauthor of two nonfiction books and a frequent conference speaker. After a ten-year business career, he returned to school to study religion and communications, earning two master's degrees. He has launched entrepreneurial enterprises in consulting and publishing and has taught in adult education for numerous years. He lives in Texas, where he works for a nonprofit organization.

www.DinnerWithAPerfectStranger.com

• Read the reviews

• Tell us what you think

• Download a reader's guide

• Meet the author

WaterBrook Press